Off

F

FAMILY NAMES
by Catherine Pelonero

CHERRY BLEND WITH VANILLA
by Le Wilhelm

AWKWARD SILENCE
by Jay Reiss

NOTHING IN COMMON
by Jennifer Fell Hayes

THE SPELLING BEE
by Phillip Vassalo

HIGHWIRE
by Brian Shields

PIZZA: A LOVE STORY
by Julianne Bernstein

A SAMUEL FRENCH ACTING EDITION

SAMUEL FRENCH
FOUNDED 1830

SAMUELFRENCH.COM
SAMUELFRENCH-LONDON.CO.UK

FOR PRODUCTION ENQUIRIES

UNITED STATES AND CANADA
Info@SamuelFrench.com
1-866-598-8449

UNITED KINGDOM AND EUROPE
Plays@SamuelFrench-London.co.uk
020-7255-4302

Each title is subject to availability from Samuel French, depending upon country of performance. Please be aware that *FAMILY NAMES, CHERRY BLEND WITH VANILLA, AWKWARD SILENCE, NOTHING IN COMMON, THE SPELLING BEE, HIGHWIRE,* and *PIZZA: A LOVE STORY* may not be licensed by Samuel French in your territory. Professional and amateur producers should contact the nearest Samuel French office or licensing partner to verify availability.

TABLE OF CONTENTS

FAMILY NAMES

by Edna Pelonero

Family Names was first produced in November, 1993 at the Nat Horne Theatre, New York City, by Love Creek Productions with the following cast:

SHEILA O'KEEFE ....Lauren Simpson

MARIE SALUZZO....................................Jennifer Hall

The production was directed by Jeff Gonzalez. The play was restaged as part of the Off-Off-Broadway Short Play Festival in April, 1994 with the same cast. Jeffrey J. Albright directed.

CHARACTERS

Sheila O'Keefe – A nervous but determined young woman.

Marie Saluzzo – A blasé young woman with a wit as sharp as a scalpel.

TIME & PLACE

The present. The office of Holiday Hardware.

This play is for Irene Tassiopulos,
Comedienne Fantastiqué
and
The Peloneros
First Family of Duplicate Names

FAMILY NAMES

SETTING: A bare office with a desk, a chair behind the desk, and a chair next to the desk, and a telephone and intercom on top of the desk.

AT RISE: MARIE is sitting at the desk doing some sort of paperwork. SHEILA enters hesitantly and looks intently at MARIE, who doesn't seem to notice her. After a moment, SHEILA takes a deep breath, works up her courage, and approaches Marie.

SHEILA. I'm looking for Marie Saluzzo.
MARIE. Yes?
SHEILA. Yes. (*Pause.*) Are you Marie Saluzzo?
MARIE. Correct for ten points.
SHEILA. Oh. Okay. Well . . . I want to have a word with you.

(Pause; MARIE does not respond.)

SHEILA. Is that okay?
MARIE. You don't see me bolting out the door, do you?
SHEILA. Okay. Well. I don't know where to begin.
MARIE. Well, I'll be here when you figure it out. (*Goes back to her work.*)
SHEILA. Look, this isn't easy for me. (*Pause.*) I want to say the right thing. Maybe I don't even have a right to be here. I just felt like I had to confront you and . . . and . . . I don't know, exactly. I just couldn't take it anymore! I had to meet you and tell you my side of it, and find out where you stand. (*Pause.*) Maybe it would be easier this way, is there anything you'd like to ask me?
MARIE. One thing, maybe.
SHEILA. Anything! I'll tell you anything.
MARIE. Who are you?

SHEILA. What? Oh, oh, well . . . I'm Sheila. Sheila O'Keefe. Does my name mean anything to you?

MARIE. No, I can't say that it does.

SHEILA. Well, I'm . . . I'm . . . look, I've just got to say this, and I hope I don't sound frantic or cold, but . . .

(PHONE rings.)

MARIE. Holiday Hardware . . . hold on. (*Loudly over intercom.*) Joe in bathroom fixtures, you have a call on line five. (*To Sheila.*) Go on.

SHEILA. Okay, well . . . you should know that . . .

(PHONE rings.)

MARIE. (*To Sheila.*) Hold on. (*Answering phone.*) Holiday Hardware . . . hold please. (*Loudly over intercom.*) Pesticides, call on line two.

SHEILA. Listen to me, please!

MARIE. All right already, I'm listening.

SHEILA. I'm . . . I'm in love with your husband! We've been having an affair for six months and we're in love. Yes, I'm the other woman. I know you must be shocked to hear this.

MARIE. Yes, quite shocked. Especially since I'm not married.

SHEILA. What? You're not . . . ? But . . . aren't you Marie Saluzzo?

MARIE. Yes.

SHEILA. Don't you have a husband named Joe?

MARIE. Not to my knowledge.

SHEILA. Isn't this Holiday Hardware?

MARIE. Yes, it is.

SHEILA. And you're Marie Saluzzo.

MARIE. Yes, I am.

SHEILA. Then how come you don't have a husband named Joe?

MARIE. Is this a trick question?

SHEILA. If your name is Marie Saluzzo, and you work here, at

Holiday Hardware, then you *must* be married to a man named Joe.

MARIE. Funny. They never mentioned that when I was hired.

SHEILA. You're telling the truth, aren't you?

MARIE. About what?

SHEILA. You don't have a husband named Joe Saluzzo.

MARIE. No.

SHEILA. You don't.

MARIE. I have a brother named Joe Saluzzo.

SHEILA. A what?

MARIE. A brother.

SHEILA. A brother? I don't understand.

MARIE. We have the same parents.

SHEILA. I know what a brother is!

MARIE. Then what part don't you understand?

SHEILA. Just let me get this straight; Joe Saluzzo is your brother.

MARIE. He's my brother.

SHEILA. You're not married to him?

MARIE. This isn't Mississippi, you know.

SHEILA. (*Takes it in for a moment.*) No-good liar!

MARIE. Fine, don't believe me.

SHEILA. I believe you; your brother is a no-good liar!

MARIE. My brother is no liar.

SHEILA. He told me you were his wife!

MARIE. My brother would never say that.

SHEILA. He most certainly did!

MARIE. He told you he was married to his sister?

SHEILA. Yes! I mean, no . . . he didn't say he was married to his sister.

MARIE. That's the truth.

SHEILA. What's the truth?

MARIE. He's not married to his sister.

SHEILA. No. He told me he had a wife named Marie, and that she works here!

MARIE. So he didn't lie.

SHEILA. But you're his sister!

MARIE. That's true.

SHEILA. So he lied!

MARIE. What did he lie about?

SHEILA. He said he had a wife named Marie and she works here.

MARIE. That's true.

SHEILA. What's true?

MARIE. He has, and she does.

SHEILA. Who has and who does?

MARIE. He has a wife named Marie and she works here.

SHEILA. You just said you're his sister.

MARIE. I am.

SHEILA. Wait a minute . . . are you telling me that you are Marie Saluzzo, and you have a brother named Joe, and he has a wife named Marie Saluzzo? In other words, there are two Marie Saluzzos, and the other one is your sister-in-law, and you both work here?

MARIE. You're quick.

SHEILA. Oh, God, oh . . . I feel like I just made a fool of myself!

MARIE. You did. (*Goes back to work.*)

SHEILA. I'm really embarrassed. And I'm really sorry, too. I am, I'm so sorry.

MARIE. Don't apologize to me.

SHEILA. I feel like I owe you an apology.

MARIE. I feel like you owe my sister-in-law an apology.

SHEILA. (*After a pause.*) So . . . is your sister-in-law here?

MARIE. Which one?

SHEILA. Marie Saluzzo!

MARIE. She's here.

SHEILA. Where could I find her?

MARIE. On the floor.

SHEILA. The floor?

MARIE. The floor of the store.

SHEILA. Oh, the floor of the store. Like, she works in the store, out on the sales floor.

MARIE. You're really catching on now.

SHEILA. I guess I should go find her.

MARIE. I wouldn't if I were you.

SHEILA. I've come this far, I might as well talk to her.

MARIE. Suit yourself.

SHEILA. What department does she work in?

MARIE. She works at the sharpening counter.

SHEILA. The "sharpening" counter?

MARIE. The sharpening counter.

SHEILA. Fine. The sharpening counter. (*Prepares to exit; hesitates and turns back.*) What does she sharpen?

MARIE. Blades.

SHEILA. Like, knife blades?

MARIE. Like, sometimes, but mostly, like, chainsaw blades.

(PHONE rings.)

MARIE. Holiday Hardware . . . hold, please. (*Very loudly over intercom.*) Marie in paint, take the call on line six.

SHEILA. I thought she worked at the sharpening counter.

MARIE. Different Marie.

SHEILA. Oh. Three Maries. That must be confusing for you.

MARIE. Not at all. I know which one I am.

SHEILA. I have no right to ask you, but what do you think . . .

(PHONE rings.)

MARIE. Holiday Hardware . . . hold please. (*Loudly over intercom.*) Joe Saluzzo, take the call on line five.

SHEILA. Joe is here?!

MARIE. Joe in lumber. My cousin.

(PHONE rings.)

MARIE. Holiday Hardware . . . hold on. (*Loudly over intercom.*) Joe in lawn & garden, the petunia man is on line six. (*To Sheila.*) Now what did you say?

SHEILA. What do you think I should do?

MARIE. Date single men.

SHEILA. You're very judgmental.

MARIE. You asked my advice.

SHEILA. You're right, I'm sorry, I have no right to be indignant. I just hate to feel like . . . an adulteress. It sounds so awful.

MARIE. It sounds better than homewrecker. Or conniving slut. Or man-stealing bitch. Or . . .

SHEILA. Fine! Adulteress sounds better. (*Pause.*) Would you please do something for me? I absolutely have to talk to your sister-in-law.

MARIE. Marie in chainsaws.

SHEILA. Yes, Marie in chainsaws. I have to do this, and I have to do it now. Do you think you could call her in here, to the office, so she and I could step outside and talk in private?

(PHONE rings.)

MARIE. Holiday Hardware . . . hold on. (*Loudly over intercom.*) Marie in paint, there's a delivery for you on the back dock. Marie in chainsaws, there's an adulteress here to see you.

SHEILA. You didn't have to do that! Forget it, I'm leaving!

MARIE. (*Over intercom.*) Cancel the adulteress.

SHEILA. This was a stupid idea anyway! I can't believe I did this! Tell your sister-in-law whatever you want, and tell your brother . . . no . . . I'll tell him myself. I'm going to do what I should have done in the first place; I'm going right over to the bakery and I'm going to tell him what he is, right in front of all his customers!

MARIE. What bakery?

SHEILA. His bakery, the . . . no, don't tell me; your brother doesn't own a bakery.

MARIE. My brother repairs air conditioners. But I have an uncle who owns a bakery, and . . .

MARIE and SHEILA. . . . his name is Joe Saluzzo.

SHEILA. Fine. Fine. Well, you tell Marie in chainsaws and Joe in lumber, and Marie in paint, and Joe your brother who repairs air conditioners that I'm really sorry for all the trouble. And if you see

Marie, the baker's wife, you can tell her that he's all hers.

(SHEILA, on the verge of a breakdown, exits. MARIE looks after her.)

MARIE. He's not married.

BLACKOUT

END OF PLAY

COSTUME PLOT

Both women wear contemporary skirts and blouses.
Sheila wears a raincoat and carries a purse.

PROPERTY PLOT

1 desk
telephone/intercom
2 chairs
pencil holder
writing paper
pen

CHERRY BLEND WITH VANILLA

by Le Wilhelm

Cherry Blend with Vanilla was originally produced under the title *Your Daddy Was a Good Man* at the Cubiculo Theatre. It was directed by Helen Diane Hoblit with the following cast:

ADA ....Ruth Sherman

BRENDA ....Linda Tvrdy

TOM..Michael Ray Martin

CHARACTERS

BRENDA

ADA

TOM

TIME & PLACE

The present. In the woods at the bank of a river.

To my mother
Lucinda Audophina Wilhelmina (Schwartz) Wilhelm
and to the memory of my father
Ernest Arthur Wilhelm

CHERRY BLEND WITH VANILLA

BRENDA. Breeze feels good.

ADA. Uh huh.

BRENDA. The sound of the river, sloshing away.

ADA. You ever been down here with it raining?

BRENDA. No . . . don't recall it, Momma.

ADA. Sound of the rain on the water, on the trees, and the grass and the sound of the river and the wind up there dancing in the leaves . . . your daddy always loved that.

BRENDA. Who wouldn't?

ADA. You'd be surprised. Some folks don't give a hoot about the river. 'Specially men.

BRENDA. Men like it down here, Momma.

ADA. Oh, they like to fish or bring their girlfriends down here at night and drink and carouse, but they don't listen to it. They don't give a tinker's damn about the wind high up in the leaves. Takes a special man to do that. Takes a good man.

BRENDA. I know, Momma.

ADA. Brenda!!

BRENDA. What?

ADA. Smell.

BRENDA. Huh?

ADA. Smell.

(BRENDA takes a strong whiff.)

ADA. Do you smell anything?

BRENDA. The water and the . . . wait . . .

ADA. Yes?

BRENDA. It smells like Cherry Blend tobacco—

ADA. With vanilla.

BRENDA. (*Sniffs.*) It does!

ADA. That's what your daddy smoked.

BRENDA. I wonder where that smell's coming from.

ADA. Maybe it's your daddy trying to tell us that he's watching over us, taking care of us.

BRENDA. Probably someone way up the river who smokes the same tobacco.

ADA. He had that special-made for himself. You know, Brenda, he was the handsomest man I think I ever saw.

BRENDA. Well, he'd have to have been to have married you.

ADA. You just say that 'cause I'm your mother.

BRENDA. No. You're a pretty woman.

ADA. Not anymore. I was when I was young, but not so much anymore. But your father, he just got handsomer as he got older. Men are like that. He's the only man I ever knew who could just take my breath away.

BRENDA. Momma!! (*SHE laughs.*)

ADA. He could! God, no one knows how much I loved him.

BRENDA. I know.

ADA. And how much I miss him.

BRENDA. I know you do, Mother, but—

ADA. I'll tell you one thing. No matter how long and how hard you look, you'll never find yourself a man as good as your daddy was.

BRENDA. Not any better.

ADA. Couldn't be. Seven years ago today, he passed over. Seven years . . . sometimes I just wish I could leave here and go be with him.

BRENDA. Don't talk that way.

ADA. I mean it. I miss him that bad.

BRENDA. But you're here, Mother, and you got to try to go on with life.

ADA. Brenda, I don't like life very much without your father here.

BRENDA. You need to get out of the house.

ADA. I get out. I go grocery shopping. I'm down here on the river.

BRENDA. You know what I mean.

ADA. If you mean I should see men, there's no way, Brenda!

BRENDA. Daddy's dead, Momma. You're alive. Don't waste your life.

ADA. I never want another man!

BRENDA. Alright, but you need to get on with your life. I was talking to Zoe Glossip's daughter.

ADA. Peggy?

BRENDA. Uh huh.

ADA. How is she?

BRENDA. She's fine. Her last kid just graduated high school. She said Zoe was feeling a little sickly.

ADA. Zoe's had a lot of sickness in her life.

BRENDA. Peggy asked if you were going to be bringing your flowers into the county fair this year.

ADA. She did?

BRENDA. Uh huh.

ADA. Why, I haven't entered the flower show since your daddy died.

BRENDA. I know.

ADA. I just don't see the point. I'm surprised anyone remembers that I used to have a bit of a green thumb.

BRENDA. She asked. Said it was going to be the biggest exhibit ever. Your dahlias are really pretty this year.

ADA. They are blooming right nice this year. That variegated one by the pump house is my favorite. It's the oddest thing. It just happened. I didn't buy the bulb or anything.

BRENDA. I imagine it'd get a blue ribbon for sure.

ADA. It probably would. But I just wouldn't enjoy myself. It's been so many years, I wouldn't know anyone there.

BRENDA. Mother, that's the silliest thing I ever heard. You'd know practically everyone.

ADA. I guess I'd know a few of them.

BRENDA. I asked Peggy to send you the entry forms.

ADA. I wish you wouldn't have done that. I just don't have the desire to do it with your daddy gone.

BRENDA. Mother, I know you loved Daddy. But it's been seven years. He's dead. You got to stop living for him. You've got to get on with your life! Daddy's never coming back!

ADA. Don't talk that way.

BRENDA. I'm sorry, but it's true, I don't believe Daddy would want you sitting around moping all the time.

ADA. Brenda, you don't understand. I was his wife.

BRENDA. And I was his daughter!

ADA. It's not the same.

BRENDA. I don't want to fight, Momma. I just think you ought to consider the flower show.

ADA. If it'll make you happy, I'll think about it.

BRENDA. Good. Momma, I'm going to go up the river to that little spring and get some watercress. Will you be okay here?

ADA. Well, of course.

BRENDA. I won't be gone but a few minutes.

ADA. You know, when I was a girl, before I's married, your daddy and I used to come here and spark. (*SHE smiles.*) You run along, honey.

(BRENDA exits. ADA sits and smiles, remembering. Then a man, TOM, enters behind her. HE is seven years younger than she is and handsome. HE lights a pipe. If it is a small theater, we smell Cherry Blend with vanilla. ADA sniffs the air, smelling the tobacco.)

TOM. You always did have a good sniffer on you, Ada.

(ADA wheels, sees him, is totally shocked out of her mind.)

ADA. Who—Oh, my God. Tom??? Tom!!! It . . . it . . . it . . . it can't be.

TOM. Can't be what, Ada?

ADA. Can't be you.

TOM. It's me.

ADA. Tom?

TOM. Yeah?

ADA. It's you . . . but how??

TOM. Now, calm yourself. Breathe slowly. Calm down or you'll give yourself a heart attack.

ADA. How?

TOM. Thought I'd drop in for a spell and pay you a visit. What is it now, six years since I died?

ADA. Seven.

TOM. Has it been that long?

ADA. Yes. (*Reaches out to touch him.*) Tom, it's so wonderful to see you.

TOM. Don't touch me, woman. You touch me, you'll get a powerful case of the shivers. Shouldn't touch someone who's crossed over.

ADA. You'll never know how much I missed you.

TOM. I got some idea, Ada. (*Takes a swig of beer which HE has brought with him.*)

ADA. Where'd you get that can of beer?

TOM. Oh, we're having ourselves a little party up there, and I brung it with me.

ADA. You drink beer up there?

TOM. Uh huh.

ADA. You never drank beer when you were alive.

TOM. Sure I did.

ADA. No, you didn't, Tom. You never touched alcohol.

TOM. That's just what you thought, Ada. I always had myself a couple of beers on Friday nights. You just didn't know it.

ADA. I'd have known.

TOM. Well, I did, and you didn't. I'd always sneak them. Figured it'd upset you. You were always kind of priggish about them kinds of things. But I always liked a good beer.

ADA. That surprises me, Tom.

TOM. Up there, they've really got some good imports, and of course, it's all free, so I get myself pretty tight at least once a week.

ADA. You're getting drunk in heaven?

TOM. It's not exactly heaven, Ada.

ADA. On, no.

TOM. It ain't hell, either. Not by a long shot. They've got some good looking women up there. Real angels.

ADA. Don't tease me like that.

TOM. I'm not teasing you, Ada. Some of the women are really hot.

ADA. I don't know if I like that.

TOM. You don't have any reason not to. When we got ourselves married, it was 'til death do us part. Well, I'm dead, and I'm a free man.

ADA. Tom!!

TOM. I'm there. You're here. We might as well have ourselves some fun.

ADA. I'll always be faithful to you, just like when you and I were alive.

TOM. Ada.

ADA. What is it?

TOM. About being faithful.

ADA. You were faithful, weren't you?!

TOM. In my fashion.

ADA. In your what? You either were faithful or you weren't. Were you?

TOM. Not exactly.

ADA. You mean you were with another woman after we were married?

TOM. Women.

ADA. Women?

TOM. Uh huh.

ADA. I don't believe you.

TOM. Believe it, Ada.

ADA. I won't.

TOM. It's the truth. No need pretending any different now that I'm dead.

ADA. You mean you made love to other women while we were married?

TOM. I didn't exactly make love to them.

ADA. You either did or you didn't!!

TOM. I don't know if I like the term "made love." I think it'd be better to say I had carnal knowledge of them.

ADA. Carnal knowledge?

TOM. Uh huh.

ADA. What does that mean?

TOM. That means we did the act, but it wasn't for love. It was for lust.

ADA. (*Flaring.*) I can't believe what I'm hearing!! You low down son of a—

TOM. Ada!!

ADA. You are!!

TOM. You were the one I loved.

ADA. Who were the bitches?! You tell me who they were, and I'll knock the piss out of those broads.

TOM. Ada!

ADA. I will!!!

TOM. You wouldn't want to do that.

ADA. The hell I wouldn't!! I'll kill the bitches.

TOM. Too many of them, Ada. You'd have the whole countryside in mourning.

ADA. How many?

TOM. I lost count.

ADA. I thought you loved me, Tom.

TOM. That's right. I did. I still do.

ADA. How can you say that when you were out bedding half the women in town?

TOM. I was always a fairly good looking man, Ada. It wasn't that I necessarily went looking for it. It just happened. And I loved you all the while.

ADA. You're not so good looking that women were just throwing themselves at you.

TOM. They thought I was. Said I just took their breath away.

ADA. And all the time I was completely devoted to you.

TOM. Didn't I give you all the loving you wanted? Didn't I?

ADA. I guess.

TOM. Ada, didn't I?

ADA. Yes. Yes, you did.

TOM. Didn't I treat you good?

ADA. Yes.

TOM. Then what's your problem?

ADA. My problem is that you were out carousing with all these damn hussies. I bet Juanita Griffin was one of them, wasn't she?

TOM. No sense talking about who it was.

ADA. Linda Flood. I bet she—

TOM. Ada, you got to understand. Men are different than women. A man's got to have a little strange once in a while.

ADA. A little what?

TOM. Strange. You know.

ADA. No, I don't know.

TOM. Variety. Give a man a little variety once in a while, and he realizes how good he has it at home. 'Cause none of those women compared to you.

ADA. If I was so good in bed—

TOM. You are, Ada.

ADA. Then why did you go around sampling—

TOM. How a man is.

ADA. And they let you do things like that up in heaven?

TOM. It isn't exactly heaven, Ada. I told you that before. But you can do what you want up there. And there's a lot of pretty women around.

ADA. And they find you breathtaking, I suppose.

TOM. Couple of them do.

ADA. (*Honestly shaken, SHE can no longer contain herself.*) I just always thought we had something special!! (*SHE is crying.*)

TOM. We did.

ADA. Then why?

TOM. I love you, Ada. I love you with all my heart. And I still remember every part of your body. The little moles on your back that made me think of a constellation. The silky hair on your stomach, and that little scar on your thigh you got—

ADA. (*Being turned on.*) Don't, Tom.

TOM. The others were just passing . . . it's all like dreams, Ada. And Tom and Ada was my special dream, and I cherished every moment of it . . . but when I was somewhere else, then other dreams—short little catnap dreams—would happen, but I always came back to our dream . . . even now up there with all those beautiful women and all the partying and dancing . . . there's lots of dancing up there, Ada . . . I still remember our dream.

ADA. I don't imagine I'd have a chance with you up there.

TOM. That all depends.

ADA. I think you're forgetting our dream.

TOM. No, I haven't.

ADA. Look at me. I've gotten seven years older since you died, and you, you haven't aged at all. In fact, I think you look younger.

TOM. It's like that. If you enjoy life and you live, then when you get up there, you're young. But if you don't . . . oh, there's some mighty ugly old shriveled people come up there.

ADA. Way I'll be.

TOM. That's up to you. Now, Ada, I love you. But if you let yourself dry up and get all ugly and don't go on living down here, I won't have anything to do with you when you pass over. 'Cause Ada, I always like my women pretty. That's why I married you.

ADA. What do you want me to do?

TOM. Quit sitting around the house all day pining over me.

ADA. You want me to go out and have intercourse with everyone like you did?

TOM. Would you like to do that, Ada?

ADA. No. My God! I don't want all the old men around here.

TOM. Whatever you want.

ADA. I want you!

TOM. I know you do, woman. But I'm not here. So you're going to have to settle for something that's second best. Ain't there a county fair coming up pretty soon?

ADA. Yeah.

TOM. You entered?

ADA. No.

TOM. Why not?

ADA. I just don't have the heart.

TOM. Find it, Ada. You know up where I am, you can gather magic dust, Ada. It's not an easy job and takes a long time to get just a smidgen of that dust. But I gathered it and sprinkled it on that dahlia by the pump house.

ADA. That variegated one that just came up without me planting it?

TOM. That's it. I did that for you, Ada. You know how Beverly

Daniels always wins the prize for best dahlia in the show? I sprinkled that magic dust on that dahlia so you could whip Beverly's ass and take home that ribbon. Never liked Beverly. She's just a little high faluting for me. But you never entered that dahlia, did you, Ada?

ADA. I didn't know about the magic. I'll enter it, Tom. I'll enter it.

TOM. And you're going to start living, right?

ADA. If I do, will you talk to me when I cross over?

TOM. Talk to you, woman? When you cross over, I plan on doing a hell of a lot more than just talking.

ADA. Tom.

TOM. Or maybe you don't want me that way anymore.

ADA. No, I want you, Tom.

TOM. Good. 'Cause I sure as hell want you, woman. Listen to the wind up there dancing in the sycamore leaves, and the river . . .

ADA. Tom, I love you, but you shouldn't have been unfaithful.

TOM. Someday you'll understand. I got to get going! Not allowed down here for too long.

(ADA rushes to him and kisses him and faints dead away.)

TOM. Woman, I told you not to do that. Kissing the dead'll clean knock you out cold.

(HE gently lies her down to rest. BRENDA enters and sees him. SHE, too, is afraid, but not as afraid as Ada was.)

BRENDA. Daddy?

TOM. Brenda, you sure grew up pretty!

BRENDA. What's wrong with Momma? Did she die?

TOM. No, she ain't dead. She just fainted. She touched me. Living get a jolt when they touch the dead.

BRENDA. What's going—

TOM. Brenda, there's not time to explain. I had to come back for a little bit because of your ma.

BRENDA. She misses you.

TOM. Tell me. That's why I'm here. She's got to pull herself together.

BRENDA. You don't drink. What are you doing with that beer?

TOM. Just a prop. Never liked the way the stuff tasted.

BRENDA. Do you think you helped her?

TOM. Maybe just a little. I 'spect she'll be getting out of the house. Might even get herself a boyfriend.

BRENDA. What did you tell her?

TOM. Just a couple of fibs. But I think she'll forgive me once she passes over and I straighten it all out.

BRENDA. What kind of things?

TOM. Private things. Things between a husband and wife. I got to go. Can only be here for a few minutes.

BRENDA. Will you come back?

TOM. I hope I don't have to. It's mighty painful for the dead when they have to pass over and speak with the living. Honey, your momma's fine. She'll come around any time now.

BRENDA. It was good to see you. (*SHE goes toward him.*)

TOM. Don't touch me, honey. You take care. I love you. (*HE exits.*)

ADA. (*Coming around.*) What's going on here?

BRENDA. I don't know.

ADA. I think your daddy was here, Brenda. Smell that Cherry Blend.

BRENDA. I smell it, Momma.

ADA. I used to think that was his only bad habit.

BRENDA. Daddy was a good man.

ADA. Yes.

BRENDA. Best man in this world.

ADA. But he was a man. Not perfect. I think I will enter my flowers at the county fair.

BRENDA. Good!

ADA. You wouldn't have any idea if Beverly Daniels still goes to the flower shows?

BRENDA. I think she won first place at the state fair last year.

ADA. Really?

BRENDA. Why?

ADA. I was just thinking that maybe she could use a little competition. That certainly is beautiful watercress. I'll make a big salad out of that for us. Maybe we'll ask Mrs. Bright over. Memory serves me, she always liked a good watercress salad.

BRENDA. Listen to the breeze way high up in the sycamore.

ADA. Lovely. (*A moment.*) But we've lollygagged enough, Brenda. I got things to do.

THE END

Author's Notes

Costumes: This play can be performed in modern day dress. The mother should dress "plain."

Property: Basket, pipe, beer

Set: The play takes place in a woods at the bank of a river, and can be done with bare stage or with trees, rocks as production budget allows.

AWKWARD SILENCE

by Jay Reiss

Awkward Silence was presented in the Off-Off-Broadway Short Play Festival by The After Hours Company. It was directed by Phil Miller. The cast was as follows:

MAN ....Ray Napoli

WOMAN..Chris Whelan

WAITER..Joseph Narciso

CHARACTERS

MAN

WOMAN

WAITER

TIME & PLACE

Present day. A restaurant.

AWKWARD SILENCE

A restaurant. A table is center. A WOMAN is stage left in SPOTLIGHT.

WOMAN. Is he short? Is he fat? Does he have nice teeth? Does he have teeth? Does he wear good shoes? Does he have hair on his head?

(A SPOTLIGHT up on the MAN, stage right.)

MAN. Does she have hair on her arms?
WOMAN. Does he have hair on his back?
MAN. Is she tall?
WOMAN. Does he live with his mother?
MAN. Is she like my mother?
WOMAN. Will he think I'm pretty?
MAN. Will she think I'm funny?
WOMAN. Does he read?
MAN. Is she republican?
WOMAN. Can he read?
MAN. Do I pay for her?
WOMAN. Is he paying for me?
MAN. Is she anemic?
WOMAN. Does he appreciate the versatility of tomatoes?
MAN. Can I trust her?
WOMAN. Will I get hurt?
MAN. Do I smell?
WOMAN. What's that smell?

(THEY move to the table.)

WOMAN. We exchange greetings.
MAN. Greetings.

39

WOMAN. Greetings.

MAN. Pleasantries.

WOMAN. Pleasantries.

MAN and WOMAN. I discreetly appraise her/his appearance.

WOMAN. And conclude that for a woman of my desperation, he passes my absolute appearance minimum.

MAN. And I give a positive approval although noting facial imperfections.

WOMAN and MAN. Followed by fabricated smiles to ease the tension.

(THEY fabricate smiles to ease the tension.)

MAN. I blindly compliment her choice of apparel.

WOMAN. I thank him, knowing he couldn't care less, and return the compliment, which I don't mean, just to be polite.

(Pause.)

MAN. Awkward silence.

WOMAN. Awkward silence.

(Pause.)

MAN. I utter a clever ice breaking remark. (*Laughs.*)

WOMAN. He says something stupid.

MAN. (*To himself.*) Was that stupid?

WOMAN. And we discuss pertinent information.

MAN. Current employment.

WOMAN. Current employment.

MAN. Dislikes of current employment.

WOMAN. General location of residence.

MAN. General location of residence.

WOMAN. Advantages to general location of residence.

MAN. We question for required standards.

WOMAN. Financial situation?

MAN. Relationship objective?

WOMAN. Financial situation?
MAN. Medical history?
WOMAN. Mental stability?
MAN. Test results?
WOMAN. Test results?
MAN. Followed by additional . . .
WOMAN. Small talk.
MAN. Small talk.
WOMAN. Small Talk.
MAN. Small talk.

(Pause.)

WOMAN. Awkward silence.
MAN. Awkward silence.

(Pause.)

WOMAN. I stare into my menu.
MAN. I avoid making eye contact.
WOMAN and MAN. Because I have nothing to say. *(Small pause.)* Awkward silence. *(Small pause.)* And then we discuss our mutual friend who set us up.
MAN. Ellen this.
WOMAN. Ellen that.
MAN. Superlative statement of Ellen's greatness.
WOMAN. Gushing agreement with said statement.
MAN. Small talk.
WOMAN. Small talk.
MAN. Small talk.
WOMAN. Small talk.

(Pause.)

MAN. I stare at the prices.
WOMAN. I say I'm thirsty.
MAN. I signal the waiter for water. *(HE does.)*

WOMAN. And I can't think of any potential conversation when luckily . . .

MAN. Blah, blah blah blah blah, blah blah blah . . .

WOMAN. He talks about himself for a half hour.

MAN. My novel blah blah blah blah . . .

WOMAN. He drops some names.

MAN. Dom Deluise blah blah blah blah . . .

WOMAN. Tells me what they did together.

MAN. Art opening blah blah blah blah . . .

WOMAN. And who they ran into.

MAN. Connie Chung blah blah blah blah. Isn't that weird?

WOMAN. Of course not, but I give a false laugh. (*SHE does.*) Noting self-indulgence.

MAN. Followed by . . .

WOMAN. Banal chatter.

MAN. Banal chatter.

WOMAN. Banal chatter.

MAN. We pause as . . .

WAITER. I pour the water. (*HE does, then exits.*)

MAN. Because we don't want him . . .

WOMAN. To overhear . . .

MAN. Our banal chatter.

(Pause.)

WOMAN. Awkward silence.

(Pause.)

MAN. I'm about to excuse myself, to use the bathroom, never to return of course, when . . .

WOMAN. Blah, blah blah blah blah . . .

MAN. She tells some long and pointless story.

WOMAN. And the elevator's broken blah blah blah blah blah, blah blah blah, blah blah blah blah . . .

MAN. I carefully place interjections to feign interest.

WOMAN. Blah blah.

MAN. Yea.

WOMAN. Blah blah.

MAN. Wow.

WOMAN. Blah blah.

MAN. Yowza. All the while wondering if it's obvious that I'm barely paying attention.

WOMAN. . . . Blah blah blah. I accuse him of not listening to me.

MAN. Which I deny, repeating the random phrases I heard back to her. Blah blah blah blah.

WOMAN. Getting the highlights, but missing the point completely.

MAN. What point?

MAN and WOMAN. Very awkward silence.

(Pause.)

MAN. What are you going to get?

WOMAN. I don't know.

(Pause.)

MAN and WOMAN. I feel uncomfortable, knowing I wish to be someplace else. Wondering why she/he doesn't like me.

MAN. Self-doubt.

WOMAN. Self-doubt.

MAN. Self-doubt.

WOMAN. Self-doubt.

MAN and WOMAN. So I conjure up a dozen airtight excuses of why I suddenly have to leave. But I don't say anything.

MAN. I think of how long it's been.

WOMAN. I think how lonely I feel.

MAN. How tired I am . . .

WOMAN. Of being alone over here . . .

MAN. When I could be over there.

MAN and WOMAN. And I wonder if a person of my romantic desperation should act like this.

WOMAN. More self-doubt.

MAN. I'm pathetic.

MAN and WOMAN. Because I know how being alone is very . . . boring.

(Pause.)

MAN. Would you like some bread?

WOMAN. Yes. Thank you.

(MAN makes gesture to Waiter for bread.)

WOMAN. I make a slight smile.

MAN. A casual glance.

WOMAN. And I lean forward . . .

MAN. Becoming interested . . .

MAN and WOMAN. In what she/he has to say.

WOMAN. We exchange parental divorce stories.

MAN. I was nine.

WOMAN. I was ten.

MAN. And as we speak . . .

WOMAN. About our childhoods.

MAN and WOMAN. I feel more relaxed.

WOMAN. And I have . . .

MAN. So much to say . . .

WOMAN. That we . . .

MAN and WOMAN. Say the same thing at the same time.

(BOTH laugh.)

MAN. I tell her to go.

WOMAN. I tell him to go.

MAN and WOMAN. And we do it again. *(More laughing.)*

WOMAN. He becomes more animated.

(MAN makes hand puppet with napkin.)

MAN. (*Puppet voice.*) I charm her with my goofiness.

WOMAN. Followed by.

MAN. Witty banter.

WOMAN. Witty banter.

MAN. Witty banter.

WOMAN. Witty banter.

MAN. I make a suggestion to continue at a location of decreased population.

WOMAN. Enthusiastic compliance.

MAN and WOMAN. As we signal the waiter for the check.

BLACKOUT

COSTUME PLOT

WOMAN: Overdressed, suit outfit.
MAN: Underdressed, casual, neat.
WAITER: Like a waiter.

PROPERTY PLOT

2 cloth napkins
2 water glasses
1 water pitcher
1 bread basket
A restaurant table for two

NOTHING IN COMMON

by Jennifer Fell Hayes

To Bryant and my Emma "elf gift"

Nothing in Common had its world premier on October 21, 1993. It was produced by Performers At Work Theatre Company at The William Redfield Theatre in New York City. The cast was as follows:

JEAN ....Patrice Grullion

CAROL..Joy Passey

Directed by: Nancy Selin
Assistant Director: Liz Haverty
Production Stage Manager: Stephen Nalewicki
Technical Director: Deirdre Howarth
Costumes Designer: Patrice Grullion, Joy Passey
Lighting Designer: Jeff Croiter
Set Designer: Nancy Sellin
Sound Designer: Nancy Sellin
Lighting & Sound Technicians: Billy Gillespie, Rhonda Merritt, Stephen Nalewicki

Nothing in Common was subsequently performed by Performers At Work Theatre Company at The 19th Annual Off-Off Broadway Short Play Festival on April 9 & 10, 1994, at The Nat Horne Theatre in New York City. The cast was as follows:

JEAN ....Patrice Grullion

CAROL..Joy Passey

Directed by: Nancy Sellin
Costumes: Patrice Grullion, Joy Passey
Prop Master: Chris Roche
Technicians: Liz Haverty, Billy Gillespie, Martha Gilpin, Andrew Jarkowsky, Kerry Prep

CHARACTERS

JEAN, mid-thirties

CAROL, sixteen

TIME & PLACE

Present day.
Jean's home, Carol's home, a hospital room.

NOTHING IN COMMON

Two women, JEAN and CAROL, are onstage in two different areas, obviously their homes, facing audience. JEAN, in her mid-thirties, is wearing smartish pants and a sweater; CAROL, about sixteen, is in a baggy tee shirt and jeans.

JEAN. We had nothing in common, really. And I only met her once—

CAROL. (*Overlapping.*) I guess you'd say I chose her—

JEAN. It was an overcast, winter day when we met. I drove to her home, some two or three hours away from the city. It was a rural, depressed area, and I had trouble finding where she lived.

I stopped in a little country town to ask directions, and got a cup of coffee in a bleak shopping mall because I was early for our appointment. Then I worried my breath would smell stale, so I bought a toothbrush and toothpaste and cleaned my teeth in the coffee shop's not very clean bathroom. I wanted her to like me so much, to choose me. I had spent a lot of time deciding what to wear the night before: I didn't want to put her off, to look too well-dressed, too smart, too alien, too intimidating, too old. Too removed from her world. And yet, perhaps, that's how she hoped I would look. I just didn't know.

CAROL. I wondered what she looked like. She was educated, I knew that. That was O.K. Sometimes I wish I'd gotten through high school, but it didn't work out for me. That was when I met Zach, and I kind of lost interest in going to class. I didn't see much point, you know? To do all my assignments, to get good grades— for what? Be a teacher, like Miss Emberley? She smelled of, you know, old sweat and was boring. Her classes were boring and she had this boring life with her boring, cranky mother. I didn't want to be like her.

JEAN. All the way there I was wondering if I should lie about my age. I'm thirty-six. The lawyer advised me to—said it would

51

put her off. I mentally chopped several years out of my life—telescoped dates—in case she asked. I hated doing it. But I wanted her to choose me—she had to, she had to. When she first phoned, in response to my ad, my heart beat so fast I—

CAROL. I thought I'd faint when I made the first call. It was real scary, you know—

JEAN. I'd been waiting for weeks and was running out of hope. Paul wasn't home from work yet and I went crazy waiting for him to arrive. He was as excited as I was, though initially he was uncertain.

CAROL. (*Overlapping.*) He wasn't, you know, certain at first. Zach, I mean. We hadn't told my mom. He thought I should, like, have an abortion, and we even went to a clinic, but they wanted money up-front and there was no way we had it. I was, like, glad. But I'd have done it, I guess. I didn't know what else to do, but I was glad I didn't have to. I knew I couldn't look after, like, a baby, though. I'd no money, Zach didn't either, and there was no way he could marry me. And I knew things weren't going to change.

Don't get me wrong! This wasn't, like, easy for me. I loved that baby, and I wanted him. I wanted him every time I felt him kick inside me. I used to say he'd be a football player, he kicked so hard! I always knew he was a boy. But what could I give him? What kind of a life could he have with me? Let's face it—I could hardly take care of myself! I didn't know what we were going to do—then I saw these ads in a local paper.

JEAN. Our lawyer told us how to advertise for a baby—it's legal in our state. We ran ads in two rural papers for several months. In the ads we gave a phone number that was for an unlisted phone we'd had installed. We called it the "baby phone." The first time it rang I was shaking so much I could hardly pick it up . . . It was a wrong number! But the next time it was Carol . . .

JEAN. (*Picks up phone, taking a huge breath.*) Hello? (*Pause.*) Hello?

CAROL. Hello? I'm calling about, you know, your ad.

JEAN. (*Holding phone tightly.*) Yes—you say you saw our ad?

CAROL. Yeah—about a baby. I'm going to have a baby, and, like, I can't keep him.

JEAN. (*With real sympathy.*) I'm so sorry. (*To audience.*) And I was very sorry, but also I was glad for me. This might be my baby . . . (*Into phone.*) We—that is, my husband and I—want a child so much, and it hasn't worked out for us. You really can't keep your baby?

CAROL. No. It's, you know, no good. I mean, like, I'm only sixteen, and so's Zach. He's, like—

JEAN. The baby's father?

CAROL. Yeah. He's, you know, not into getting married.

JEAN. He's very young.

CAROL. Yeah. What's your name?

JEAN. Jean. What's your's?

CAROL. Carol. (*To audience.*) I liked the sound of her voice. She sounded, like, O.K. Hers wasn't the first ad I picked—I liked another ad better, but when I called some guy answered and asked me, "How much do you want for it?" You can't buy my baby, I yelled at him. It's a human life you're talking about, not, like, a used car! And I slammed the phone down. (*To Jean.*) What do you do?

JEAN. I'm a graphic artist. I illustrate children's books.

CAROL. (*To audience.*) It sounded like a neat thing to do. Books for kids I liked that. We talked for a while and it felt, like O.K. (*To Jean.*) I'd like to meet you—and your husband. Could you, you know, come up here for a visit or something?

JEAN. I kept thinking, this might be my baby, and I was aware of my heart beating, beating, beating. I'd wanted a baby for so long—so many false hopes when a period was late: so many tests; so much surgery. I got to a point where it was difficult to see friends who were having babies—even babies on TV would make me cry. Sometimes my own drawing for kids' books could upset me. I remember one day when I was drawing a series of little children for a counting book, and I'd just got my period, six tantalizingly hopeful days late. There I was, lovingly etching in chubby cheeks and limbs, small fingers, little ears, while I felt the dull aching drag, the heavy flow of first day menstruation, tangible failure of my ability to create a child who was flesh and blood, not ink and paper.

To be so close to the possibility of a baby was overwhelming, so when she suggested we meet the day after next, I agreed immediately. The lawyer said if we wanted to meet her it was our affair, he wouldn't have anything to do with it. Then Paul came home and said he had to go to California the next day. There was no way he could get out of it: he'd lose an important contract if he didn't. We didn't want to change the meeting time—perhaps she might decide to see someone else. Paul had a long talk with her on the phone and it went pretty well, and she said she'd like to go through with the meeting anyway, and see me. I felt I could handle it, so a few days later I drove up. (*Rings DOOR BELL.*)

CAROL. (*Answers door.*) Hi.

JEAN. Hi. I'm Jean. I hope I'm not—

CAROL. (*Overlapping.*) Come in. (*Lets her in.*) Want to take your coat off?

JEAN. Thanks.

CAROL. (*Takes coat, hangs it up.*) Did you find it O.K.?

JEAN. (*Overlapping.*) I got a little lost at the end, that turn-off from the main road was . . .

CAROL. Yeah, it can be a hassle if you don't know . . .

JEAN. (*Overlapping.*) It wasn't a problem, really.

(*Pause.*)

CAROL. Wanna sit down?

JEAN. Sure. Here—I brought you some flowers . . .

CAROL. Oh. Thanks. I'll, you know, just . . . (*Exits.*)

JEAN. (*To audience.*) I wanted to bring her something, and agonized over what it should be—flowers, chocolates, a cake—stupid really, to make such a big deal out of it, but it *was* a big deal.

(*CAROL re-enters with the flowers stuck in a vase. SHE is uncertain what to do with them, and then sets them on a table.*)

CAROL. They're real pretty. Thanks. (*SHE sits.*)

(Pause.)

JEAN. How are you feeling?

CAROL. *(Simultaneously.)* Did you have any questions?

JEAN. Go ahead—

CAROL. No, you—

JEAN. Tell me why you can't keep your baby.

CAROL. How am I going to keep him? I told you, Zach isn't into getting married. He's leaving for California next month, wants to try his luck there. I've got no money, and I just don't want to wind up a single mom always rushing around like my friend Becky. And a kid with no dad? Forget it—I know too many. I want my kid to have a real family. *(Pause. CAROL fiddles with a bracelet.)*

JEAN. *(Picks up photo frame.)* Is this you?

CAROL. Yeah—when I was two. *(Grins.)* Cute, wasn't I?

JEAN. *(Studies photo.)* Very cute. *(Sets frame down, feels in purse.)* I brought a few photos with me—to sort of give you an idea how we live. *(To audience.)* I'd thought—if it were me trying to find a home for my baby, what would I want to know about this woman? And I thought photos of my home might help—nothing specific, nothing that would reveal our whereabouts. The lawyer told me to give her my first name only, and no address.

CAROL. *(Looks at photos.)* You live in the city, right?

JEAN. Yes.

CAROL. I don't like the city.

JEAN. It's not so terrible as it's made out. And we have a nice apartment—that's our living room.

CAROL. Where's this? With all the trees?

JEAN. It's a place we go to in the country.

CAROL. Would the baby go there?

JEAN. Yes.

CAROL. *(Looks at photo and then grins.)* You wouldn't like to adopt me, too, would you?

JEAN. *(Laughs. Then to audience.)* I wanted to say—I wish I could. She wasn't much more than a child herself. *(Shows her another photo.)* This is Paul, my husband.

CAROL. What's he do?

JEAN. He works in advertising.

CAROL. Oh. (*To audience.*) He looked O.K. Suit and tie. You know. Nothing exciting. (*Goes to tape recorder and puts in cassette. To Jean.*) Do you like Vanilla Ice? [*Substitute whatever is up-to-date.*]

JEAN. I don't know, I never heard them before.

CAROL. Him, not them!

JEAN. Oh. You like music, then?

CAROL. Yeah. I like dancing—there's a club we go to on the weekends. (*Looks down at herself.*) I haven't been there much, lately—(*Sings a bit of the song.*) when I was at school I was in a band with two of my girlfriends. We called ourselves the Blue Angels. We, you know, dyed our hair blue, and wore blue lipstick, blue nail polish. We thought we were real cool!

JEAN. Sounds fun.

CAROL. Yeah. It was great. That's what I'd like to do—be a rock star. Everyone says I have a great voice.

JEAN. What happened to the band?

CAROL. Oh, we, you know, busted up. Zach was glad, really. He, like, got pissed off waiting around.

JEAN. Would you marry Zach if you could?

CAROL. No way! (*Becomes confidential.*) If I'm honest, I *might* like to keep the baby. Be, you know, married and a mom. All that. But then I think of the rest of my life, and I know it wouldn't work for me. I know I'm not, like educated the way you are, but I know some things. And I've seen how hard it is for my friend Becky. She doesn't have any fun, she's always working. And anyway, Zach's off to California. I think he's shit scared I'll keep the baby, and he'll have to support us. So there's no way. I've got to find a good home for the baby.

JEAN. Why didn't you go to an agency?

CAROL. Because I wouldn't know anything about where he went. I wanted to be able to choose myself. I could do that for him, at least. (*A beat.*) Why can't you have one of your own?

JEAN. (*Gets up and looks out window.*) I had an ectopic pregnancy a few years ago. That's when the fetus gets stuck in the

Fallopian tube. I nearly died. I lost the right ovary and the Fallopian tube. I've had all the tests, and tried everything, but I've never been able to get pregnant again.

CAROL. Is there still a chance you might get pregnant? See, if I let you have my baby, and then you have one yourself, you might not want mine any more. Or you might treat mine, you know, differently. I don't want that for him.

JEAN. It's unlikely that I will ever get pregnant again, but if I did, I would love your baby as much as any biological child I might have.

CAROL. But maybe you're saying that so I'll decide to give you the baby. How do I know if you're telling the truth?

JEAN. You don't, I guess. You don't know me, and you don't know if I tell the truth. (*Sits down.*) How are your instincts?

CAROL. Well, my instincts got me pregnant, didn't they? (*THEY laugh. CAROL gets up.*) Hey, I'm, you know, starving. Want to go get some pizza?

JEAN. O.K. (*To audience.*) I didn't really want pizza. I was far too keyed up to eat. But I went with her to a little pizza joint a few blocks away. We sat in a booth with peeling vinyl seats, a jukebox blaring loudly, and shared a medium pie, with onions and green peppers, her choice.

(*THEY sit as if in booth.*)

CAROL. Want a Coke?

JEAN. Sure. But look—I want to pay for this.

CAROL. No way. This is, like my treat. You came all this way to see me!

JEAN. I'd like to pay. Really.

CAROL. Forget it.

JEAN. Well, I don't think it's . . .

CAROL. I said, forget it. (*Takes big bite.*) Pretty good, huh? I like the way they make the crust here. Oh, shit. (*Wipes shirt.*)

JEAN. Here, put some cold water on it. Tomato stains. (*Dips her napkin in water glass, dabs Carol's shirt.*)

CAROL. (*Embarrassed.*) Thanks. (*Watches Jean dabbing*

mark.) You didn't, like have to . . .

JEAN. (*Overlapping.*) There, just a bit more water, and it's nearly . . .

CAROL. (*Interrupts.*) Jean, like, how old are you?

JEAN. (*Deciding to tell truth.*) I'm thirty-six. (*Takes neat bites of pizza.*)

CAROL. (*Considering.*) That's good. I think, you know, you're a lot more ready to look after a child at that age than at mine. You like, know more about life. (*Sips her Coke.*)

JEAN. I guess so. Carol, it's against my interests to say this, because I desperately want to have a child, but are you really sure about this? Because years from now you might regret it. Or when you've given birth, and see this baby, you might want to change your mind.

CAROL. (*To audience.*) I couldn't, like, believe she said that. It was so nice. I felt she was, you know, really thinking about me and the baby, and not like just what she wanted. (*To Jean. Picks up salt shaker and fiddles with it.*) I'm not like, dumb, you know. I was there for Becky all through her bad time, and I held her baby when she was one day old. And I've, like, looked at her baby a lot lately and you know, thought of mine. It'll be rough—yeah. Like I said, I'm not dumb. I know that. But I can't keep this baby. No way. All I can do for him is have him—and give him away to some one who'll like, really love him, and really care for him. (*Knocks over salt picks some up, and sprinkles it over her left shoulder.*) My grandmother does that! She's like, real superstitious. I don't believe in all that stuff but I do it anyway.

JEAN. What do you want for him?

CAROL. (*Takes paper napkin from holder and folds it repeatedly.*) For him to be happy. For him to have a real family, a father and a mother who love him, take care of him, spoil him a little—you know. And for him like, to have a chance to grow up and do something he enjoys—to have, like, a good life. That's what I want for him. (*Pause. SHE begins to shred napkin into tiny pieces.*) I didn't, like, have that great a childhood. Dad left us when I was four or five, and Mom has had, you know, quite a few boyfriends since then. She did her best for me, I guess. There was always food on the table, and I had, like, enough clothes and things. And she gave me, like, nice birthdays with cake and presents and stuff. But I never felt like I had a real family. And things haven't turned out that great for me so far. I don't want that for him. And when this is over, I'm, like, you know, going to get it together. Have a fresh start. (*SHE scoops napkin shreds into a ball and drops it on her plate.*)

JEAN. (*Reaches over and touches her hand.*) I hope it works out for you, Carol, I really do.

CAROL. Yeah. Well. Listen—I appreciate you coming out here.

JEAN. I'm glad I came here. I'm really glad I got a chance to meet you. I'm sure you'll want some time to think about this, so maybe I'll hear from you in a couple of days?

CAROL. No. I decided before you came it wouldn't be fair for you to go away not knowing, and that I'd like, tell you whichever way it was going to be. And I've decided I like you, and I'd like you and your husband to be the parents of my baby.

(*THEY embrace.*)

JEAN. (*Weeping, whispers.*) Thank you.

(*THEY release each other.*)

CAROL. (*Pats her stomach.*) I could, almost like introduce you, couldn't I?

(*JEAN smiles, nods, unable to speak. CAROL gets up to leave, and JEAN watches her go.*)

JEAN. (*To audience.*) I never saw her again. I spoke to her on the phone regularly, though, and we paid for all her doctor's visits through an escrow account with our lawyer. The day Tommy was born I spoke to her for the last time.

(*SHE picks up phone, and so does CAROL.*)

CAROL. I want you to know you are the parents of a beautiful little son. (*SHE stops, choked with emotion.*)

(*JEAN cannot speak—weeps.*)

CAROL. Jean?

JEAN. Yes. (*A pause.*) I'm sorry—I'm just—Carol? Are you all right?

CAROL. Yeah. I'm, like, a little—you know.

JEAN. Yes.

CAROL. I'm not changing my mind, Jean. You know that. I'm like following my instincts!

JEAN. Was the birth . . .

CAROL. It was awesome! Longer than I'd like, though. But it's all over now. I got to see him for a little while, and he's beautiful. (*Pause.*) He weighs six pounds eight ounces. (*Pause.*) Jean?

JEAN. Yes?

CAROL. What's his room going to look like?

JEAN. It's light and airy—there's a big window with white curtains that have blue ducks and yellow elephants on them—and his crib is near the window. It's white-painted wood, with blue bumpers and bedding that has yellow and white clowns and animals on. There's a large changing table in one corner, a diaper bag that looks like a rainbow, and a white chest of drawers with a teddy bear sitting on it that Paul's parents got him already. Oh, and there's a small white bookcase with some old children's books of mine on it, and some of the books I've illustrated. And an illustration I did of a little boy climbing a tree is framed on the wall near the changing table. Paul went out and got a huge heart balloon and tied it to the crib. Does—does that give you an idea?

CAROL. (*Quietly.*) Yeah. (*Pause.*) When do you get to see him?

JEAN. The hospital says we can get him in two days. It seems like a long wait.

CAROL. Funny—we're like, in the same boat. Both the mother with no baby.

JEAN. Yes. (*Pause.*) Carol?

CAROL. Yeah?

JEAN. You know we're going to love and cherish this baby all our lives? You do know how much he means to us?

CAROL. Yes. I know.

JEAN. (*To audience.*) And she did know. And we had, for a moment, a perfect communication, a minute of real understanding between two people. Even though, as I said before, we really had nothing in common.

THE END

COSTUME PLOT

JEAN: Dress pants , dressy sweater, coat or jacket
shoes, purse

CAROL: blue jeans, oversized shirt, tennis shoes,
bathrobe

SET LIST

CAROL'S HOME: Loveseat, coffee table, small corner
table

JEAN'S HOME: Drafting table and stool or desk and
chair

PIZZA JOINT SCENE: Restaurant booth with peeling
vinyl seats or Table, two chairs with peeling vinyl seats

FINAL TELEPHONE SCENE: Small corner table and
chair— (Carol in hospital room.)

PROPERTY PLOT

ONSTAGE PROPS

JEAN
Telephone (on drafting table or desk)
Bouquet of flowers (on drafting table or desk)
Graphic paper (on drafting table or desk)
Pencils (on drafting table or desk)
Coat or jacket (on back of chair)
Purse (hanging on chair under coat or jacket)
Pictures of Paul and home (in purse)

CAROL
Coke (1 can or bottle on coffee table)
Tape player (small corner table)
Tapes (small corner table)
Picture frame with picture of Carol at two years old (on coffee table)
Small town newspaper (on coffee table)
Telephone (on coffee table)

PIZZA JOINT SCENE
Medium pizza with green peppers and onions
Two glasses of water
Two Cokes (cans)
Red & white checked plastic/paper table cloth
Napkins
Salt and pepper shakers

FINAL TELEPHONE SCENE (Carol in hospital room area)
Telephone on small table
Bathrobe on chair

OFFSTAGE PROPS

CAROL
Old glass vase or jar with water

GROUND PLOT

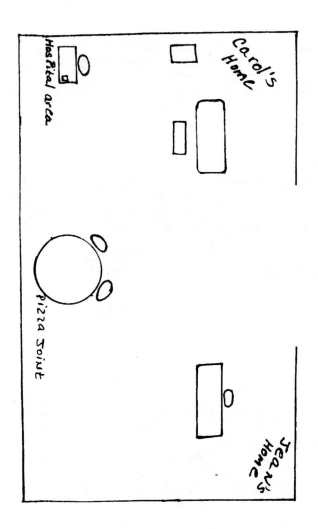

THE SPELLING BEE

by Philip Vassallo

To my father, Frank Vassallo

The Spelling Bee was originally presented by West Dog Rep, the resident company of The Hamlet of Bank Street Theatre, on December 12, 1993 at the Village Gate, New York City, and then on April 4, 1994 at the Nat Horne Theatre with the following cast:

WHITE MAN ....Joseph Amorando

BLACK MAN ....Theo Scott

Natalya Sokiel was the director and Cathie Crozier was the assistant director.

CHARACTERS

WHITE MAN – Late twenties, dressed informally.

BLACK MAN – Late twenties, similar size as WHITE MAN, also dressed informally.

TIME

The present.

THE SPELLING BEE

SCENE: DARKNESS. The WHITE MAN stands at extreme LEFT and the BLACK MAN stands at extreme RIGHT.

AT RISE: LIGHT goes up on the WHITE MAN. HE addresses the audience. As he speaks, the BLACK MAN stands in the DARKNESS and looks alternately at WHITE MAN and audience.

WHITE MAN. I got these two places. One's in Perugia. I've never been there, but my father raised me with stories about it. It's an ancient village smack in the middle of Italy in the Umbria region. It's set on a beautiful hill overlooking groves of fig and olive trees that get covered with dust every time a truck hauling fruit passes by kicking up the dry soil. And the people: They're cultured and intelligent. Not like farmers at all. But they don't throw it in your face either. Real friendly. Welcome you into their house any time of day.

My place in Perugia belonged to my family ever since my great-grandfather built it in nineteen-o-two. Whenever my father talks about that place, he never refers to it as *his* house. He calls it *"your* house." (*Smiles, pointing to himself.*) *My* house. As if I was born and bred there. I gotta see the place with my own eyes some day. I'll tell you more about my place in Perugia later. My other place is in The Bronx. As soon as I say it, most of my friends panic. They're from the Island or Jersey and to them The Bronx is some place where *their* parents grew up but have no desire to go back to because nothing's there anymore. No way they're ever gonna accept an invitation to my house. But I'm used to The Bronx. I been living here my whole life. Born in Jacobi Hospital up on Pelham Parkway and living a couple blocks from there ever since. It was the only house my parents ever had in America. They moved back to Perugia about five years ago and left the house to me and my sister. My sister's dead now . . . but that's another story . . . so I'm living alone in this big house. Right off Morris Park Avenue. Brick. Two-story detached colonial with three bedrooms upstairs, full attic and basement, flower box in the front and a small garden patch in the back. Only it's not a garden no more. I cemented it over because the roots from the tree and all them weeds was a pain in the ass to take care of. When my parents came up to visit, my mother was real pissed off. She said:

(LIGHTS up on the BLACK MAN, who mimics the White Man's mother:)

BLACK MAN. You killa my garden! *(Chuckles.)*
WHITE MAN. *(Turns to Black Man, peeved.)* You don't come in here.
BLACK MAN. *(Doubles over.)* I just had to say it. You killa my garden!
WHITE MAN. You wanna be a clown?
BLACK MAN. Just playing with you.
WHITE MAN. You want me to break in on you like that?
BLACK MAN. Take it light, man.
WHITE MAN. I can't. This is serious.
BLACK MAN. Then get serious.
WHITE MAN. If you let me, I will.
BLACK MAN. Go ahead. Sorry.
WHITE MAN. *(To audience.)* So when they came over, my mother said: *(Mimics them:)* "You killa my garden!"
"Itsa not your garden no more," my father told her. But just when I think he's on my side, *he* gets on my case. "When you gonna pointa the bricks like I tell you to?"
"Give him the money and maybe he do it," my mother says.
"Itsa his house," he says.
"Then shutta you mouth," she tells him, but right on the heels of that she says, "All the cement he shoulda used for pointing he used to bury my garden."
(Shrugs.)
Since my sister died last winter . . . because a *nigger* murdered

her for her pocketbook . . . (*A beat.*) Now I don't use the word *nigger* lightly. To me a nigger is a savage that's black. Just like a savage that's white is white trash. I wouldn't call a self-respecting, law-abiding black man a nigger just like I wouldn't call a self-respecting, law-abiding white man white trash. But I don't get bent outta shape for one second about using the word nigger—not since my sister was stabbed in her chest seven times by that nigger.

Anyway, since she died, my parents've never come back. The memories are too much, they say. For the same reason, I can't ever leave.

(LIGHT dims on the WHITE MAN. The BLACK MAN addresses the audience and the WHITE MAN stands motionless in the DARKNESS and looks alternately at BLACK MAN and audience.)

BLACK MAN. I remember the first time I walked down Morris Park Avenue. The state opened a methadone clinic at Bronx Psychiatric Hospital and I got this job there as an aide. I always took the Twenty-six bus to work from my house on Tremont and Morris Park.

WHITE MAN. (*In darkness.*) How'd you get the job?

BLACK MAN. (*Turns to White Man.*) My mother told me about it. So one day . . .

WHITE MAN. And how'd she know about it?

BLACK MAN. Yo, whose turn is it?

WHITE MAN. Just trying to help.

BLACK MAN. How you figure you trying to help?

WHITE MAN. Trying to make your story more interesting.

BLACK MAN. How my mother knew about the job ain't got nothing to do with the story.

WHITE MAN. Okay, man. If you're uptight . . .

BLACK MAN. Uptight? Shit! I ain't uptight 'bout my mother. I'm uptight about your sorry ass cutting into me like that.

WHITE MAN. Sorry.

BLACK MAN. No you ain't. (*To audience.*) My mother knew about the job because she was going to the methadone clinic for treatment. (*A beat.*) Like I was saying, I always took the Twenty-six to work. That bus goes clear across Morris Park. You start on one end near the Hundred Eightieth Street train station where the Puerto Ricans and black people live and the hoes be hustling you for fifteen dollars and then you pass the white area where you got parks, all kinds of stores, and big-assed houses. You couldn't see two worlds this fast if you was on a spaceship. (*A beat.*) Anyway, this one day I'm walking out the door and my brother Willie asked me for some money so I passed him five dollars. After he cut out I realized I didn't have no money left to take the bus so I had a walk it all the way. That's a long-assed walk in the summer. And it was already ninety degrees by eight in the morning so I was sweating like a dog. The last half a the walk is the worse, man. That's where everything turns from black to white. You know everybody's looking at me. Them old ladies coming outta those Italian delis. The white boys looking bad sitting in their convertibles with their slicked-back hair and tattoos. Shit! I thought I was in Alabama during the days of segregation. (*Chuckles.*) Alabama. Sounds Italian, don't it? (*Makes a patented Italian hand gesture and mimics:*) A-la-ba-ma, mama mia. (*A beat.*) Looked around saw a sea of white faces and I couldn't swim in it nohow. (*HE mimes the following scene.*) All a sudden this little white faggot come up to me.

(*LIGHTS up on WHITE MAN, who mimes the scene. The two men have clearly rehearsed this scene.*)

WHITE MAN. Excuse me, sir.

BLACK MAN. (*Sardonically.*) Sir! Who he kidding! I just keep walking. And this faggot keep following me.

WHITE MAN. May I ask you something?

BLACK MAN. "I gotta get to work," I tell him. Then he reaches for my arm and I shake him off real good. "Get out my way. I'm late." I shook him off like a fly. I knew I could kick this cracker's ass if I had to. But look where I was, man: Morris Park Avenue! So I just keep moving on. And he keeps following me.

WHITE MAN. Please, sir, all I want is a moment of your time.

BLACK MAN. Now I'm still at least ten blocks from the job. If I show him I'm a scared, that's the end of my ass. Who knows if I'm being set up? (*Mimes this.*) So I decide I gotta make a stand. I stop, stare him right in the eye and say, "What you want?" And he says real serious and all:

WHITE MAN. Do you live here?

BLACK MAN. It your business?

WHITE MAN. I'm asking because I'm conducting a survey . . .

BLACK MAN. I don't wanna know. Just get out my way.

WHITE MAN. . . . on the ethnic demographics of this community . . .

BLACK MAN. That's your business.

WHITE MAN. . . . and I'd like your perspective about the neighborhood's racial attitudes.

BLACK MAN. Then I say, "You mess with me I'm a fuck you up." That's when a bunch a wop-dago-greasy-assed guineas come outta one a them cappuccino shops. Must a been at least ten a them. One was carrying a baseball bat. I coulda run to my job so fast that I woulda beat Carl Lewis, Jim. But before I could move they was already surrounding me. The one with the baseball bat say:

(*The WHITE MAN now mimes the scene with a bat in his hand. HE assumes the tough demeanor and deeper voice of a hitter:*)

WHITE MAN. This man bothering you?

BLACK MAN. (*To White Man.*) No. (*As narrator:*) I'm shaking like a leaf and I know they know I know it.

WHITE MAN. Then why you threatening him?

BLACK MAN. I wasn't threatening nobody.

WHITE MAN. Looked like that to me.

BLACK MAN. Always do. That's why I'm me and you you and the world go round too. (*As narrator:*) So I turn to the faggot. "Was I threatening you?" But the faggot just stood there with his tongue hanging outta his mouth. Like he was scared too. Then I said to him, "Why you ask me that?"

WHITE MAN. What he ask you?

BLACK MAN. "Let him tell you," I say, but he start twisting the bat in his hand like he can't wait no more to use it so I say, "He asked me what about racial attitudes." Then they all stood there real quiet in this circle around me. Nobody say nothing for a long time. All I can hear is me breathing heavy. It was so quiet I could hear my own heart beat. Finally they all started laughing. (*WHITE MAN starts laughing.*) Slapping each other five and rolling all over the sidewalk and shit. Then the cracker with the bat said:

WHITE MAN. What's so bad about that? This man here is a sociology professor at Bronx Community College. You know what sociology is?

BLACK MAN. I know what sociology is. (*As narrator:*) How can a black man living in America not know what sociology is? Without the black man there'd *be* no sociology.

WHITE MAN. (*Out of the street character:*) I bet you're gonna say next that a black man invented sociology.

BLACK MAN. Would've if the white man gave him a chance.

WHITE MAN. (*Annoyed.*) Alright. Go on with your story.

BLACK MAN. (*Prompting.*) You were saying . . .

WHITE MAN. Huh?

BLACK MAN. You were being that stupid-ass cracker talking sociology.

WHITE MAN. Yeah. (*Back as street character.*) You know sociology huh? Well that's this man's business. He's doing a study on why Italians don't move from The Bronx. I hope he don't decide it's because guineas and niggers are really brothers. (*WHITE MAN laughs and steps aside with a sweeping hand gesture.*)

BLACK MAN. They let me walk on by. But I didn't go to my job. I went right back the other way. I figured if I walk through their turf, they always know where to find me, but if I go back where I came from, they ain't never gonna follow me there. So I quit my job. All because some faggot white professor couldn't mind his own goddam business. Why he gotta go asking me questions he already know the answer to? Shit! Nobody see me asking no white man about his racial attitude. I don't need to ask to know what that's all about. All I need is these two eyes. And

Stevie Wonder don't even need that! I don't wanna get nowhere near white attitudes if I could help it. Only this one time . . . I couldn't help it. I was *there*, brother.

(LIGHT dims on the BLACK MAN. The WHITE MAN addresses the audience.)

WHITE MAN. I wasn't exactly what you'd call an ace student. C-pluses, an occasional D and a B every now and then. The only thing I ever got an A in was spelling. Let's put it this way: I never got no recognition for my brains.

But one night at the dinner table I was watching the *Eyewitness News*. They had this story about this eleven-year old kid who won the national spelling bee. I'll never forget the word he won on: noesis. N-O-E-S-I-S. Six letters, three syllables. When they asked him how he felt about winning, he sounded like a real jerk. Couldn't even put a sentence together. The kid could spell like a whiz but other than that he was a dummy.

That's when it dawned on me: even *I* had some talent. I was just like that kid on the *Eyewitness News*: same age, same grade, same dummy, but a damn good speller.

I don't know why, but that story inspired me. I guess it was because you never see no kid your own age—I mean like eleven—on the news unless they got some weird disease or they murdered their kid sister with their father's hunting rifle.

Anyway, after watching the show, I busted my ass memorizing all the words on the seventh and eighth grade spelling lists. And when I got them down, I jumped to the high school list. It became like a game after a while. There wasn't a word that could stump me and finally I made it to the finals of my class spelling bee. There was just me and this black kid left. He wasn't much of a student either, but he was a good speller too. *(A beat.)* Now I'm not trying to make a bigger deal out of this than it is. It was just the finals for my *class*. But the winner would go to the school finals and then there's the district and so on right up to the nationals and the *Eyewitness News*. I zipped through at least twenty words. Capitulate: C-A-P-I-T-U-L-A-T-E. Capitulate. Quagmire: Q-U-A-

G-M-I-R-E. Quagmire. Satellite: S-A-T-E-L-L-I-T-E. That was the first time in my life I ever believed that sentence my parents hammered into my head: If you work hard you'll succeed.

(BOTH MEN transform into sixth grade students standing at attention.)

WHITE MAN. "Abstemious. A-B-S-T-E-M-I-O-U-S. Abstemious."

BLACK MAN. "Jeopardy. J-E-O-P-A-R-D-Y. Jeopardy."

WHITE MAN. "Paucity. P-A-U-C-I-T-Y. Paucity."

BLACK MAN. "Caricature. C-A-R-*(Strains in concentration.)* C-A-R-I-*(Hangs head dejectedly.)*

WHITE MAN. *(Out of child character.)* No way! No way was I gonna win this one just on some technicality, just because he repeated himself. Bullshit! I wanted to get his ass on a word that stumped him. *(Back in child character, raises hand.)* Mrs. Hunter, can he have another chance? *(A beat.)* Thank you.

BLACK MAN. "Caricature. C-A-R-I-C-A-T-U-R-E. Caricature."

WHITE MAN. "Mannequin. M-A-N-N-E-Q-U-I-N. Mannequin."

BLACK MAN. "Reinforce. R-E-I-N-F-O-R-C-E. Reinforce."

WHITE MAN. *(Out of child character.)* What is this? He's getting all the easy words. "Plethora. P-L-E-T-H-O-R-A. Plethora."

BLACK MAN. "Acquaintance."

WHITE MAN. *(Out of child character.)* Acquaintance! See what I mean?

BLACK MAN. "A-C-Q-U-A-N-T-A-N-C-E. Acquaintance."

WHITE MAN. *(Raises hand.)* He got it wrong! *(A beat. Nods his head furiously.)* Yes he did!

BLACK MAN. Okay. "Acquaintance. A-C-Q- . . . U-A-I-N-T . . . A-N-C-E. Acquaintance."

WHITE MAN. That's not fair. He had two chances! He left out the *i* the first time . . . Yes he did . . . I'm not a bad sport . . . I apologize. *(Out of child character.)* Why bother putting us up

there? Just call him the winner. (*Back in child character.*)
"Posthumous. P-O-S-T-H-U-M-O-U-S. Posthumous."

BLACK MAN. "Guarantee. G-U-A-R-A-N-T-E-E. Guarantee."

WHITE MAN. (*Out of child character.*) Man, was the deck
stacked against me! (*Back in child character.*) "Ferocious. F-E-R-
O-C-O . . . I-O. (*Looks to Black Man for support.*)

BLACK MAN. (*Ignoring him.*) "Ferocious. F-E-R-O-C-I-O-U-
S. Ferocious!" (*Freezes with a brilliant boyish smile as LIGHTS
dim on him.*)

WHITE MAN. He didn't give me the same break I gave him! I
looked at Mrs. Hunter square in the eye hoping she'd give me at
least one chance. He had two. Plus the easier words. (*A beat.*)
Ferocious! The easiest word she gave me and I blew it. (*A beat.*)
What difference did it make? She wanted him to win. Know why?
Because he was black and she didn't want a white kid to be
smarter than a black kid on that stage in front a all them white kids.
I was her scapegoat. But I spoke out! I let her know she was
cheating for him! My father always said, "Tell a cheat he's a cheat
to his face." What did it get me? I lost! (*A beat. With a sardonic
chuckle.*) The funny thing is to this day I can't spell for shit.

*(LIGHT dims on the WHITE MAN as the BLACK MAN addresses
   the audience.)*

BLACK MAN. I went to Bronx Community College. Couldn't
cut it for a semester. They be preaching all this jive about cultural
diversity in America. Damn! Just when black people are finally
going to college to learn all that good bullshit that whites keeped
for themselves all those years, now we get there and they stopped
teaching *real* subjects. All they do is talk about cultural diversity.
That ain't no subject, man. Anyway, it ain't one nobody's learning.

You know who I had for sociology? Got that right. The faggot
from Morris Park. But he didn't remember me. Guess we all look
alike to him.

*(LIGHTS up on the WHITE MAN who assumes the character of the
   professor.)*

BLACK MAN. He weren't no older than me but he acted like he been around the world and back twice over. He was a pisser.

WHITE MAN. So this *shared* community we seek to build is one reflective of the cultural wealth America enjoys.

BLACK MAN. Yo, man. Why you use the word *wealth* when talking 'bout culture?

WHITE MAN. Because of the multiplicity of *meaning* that any member of a diverse society can extract from the different cultures contained within it.

BLACK MAN. Say what?

WHITE MAN. The tribal rituals. The contrasting values. How do they contribute to the common culture? What do they mean? Even the simplest of colloquial expressions. Consider the ways the students in this class address me. This speaks volumes about our cultural identity. (*Points.*) Rodrigo is a Colombian newly arrived in America. He addresses me as "Professor." (*Points.*) And Kim here is fresh from Taiwan. She calls me "Sir." (*Points.*) And Brian, a third generation Irish-American says, "Mr. DiBlasi" when speaking to me. And you're an African-American and you call me "Yo man."

BLACK MAN. What's that supposed to mean?

WHITE MAN. What, "yo man"? *You* tell me.

BLACK MAN. I think you playing with me.

WHITE MAN. Why do you think that?

BLACK MAN. Because you never taught no multiculturalism until them Asians came here. You ain't never gonna include the black man unless you throw him in with the whole lot of Chinese, Japanese, Burmese, and Vietnamese coming off the boat.

WHITE MAN. (*Turns to Black Man, out of professor character, annoyed.*) Whoa!

BLACK MAN. Now we supposed to fit in with all these Asians we got nothing to do with. It used to be the white man up here (*Raises his hand above his head.*) and the black man down here. (*Lowers the same hand below his knee.*) Now the black man's been demoted even lower. (*Stamps his foot as if squashing something.*)

WHITE MAN. Where's all this coming from?

BLACK MAN. Can't find us no more unless you go past Chinatown and the Barrio and Little Russia. Now we lumped in with *all* the cultures. But you ain't. It's still the white man and everybody else. Shit, before multiculturalism at least we was niggers. Now we just lost in the crowd.

WHITE MAN. You didn't tell your professor that.

BLACK MAN. Shut up, man.

WHITE MAN. No I won't!

BLACK MAN. You know what all that shit is. Just another way to tell me how to think.

WHITE MAN. Your own people have demanded that that be taught.

BLACK MAN. What my-own-people? I ain't got no own people!

WHITE MAN. You can't have it both ways. You can't ask for black leaders and then when they get into power say they ain't your leaders.

BLACK MAN. Why not? How many whites willing to say Hitler's their leader? I can say whatever nasty shit I wanna say about any man, be he black or white.

WHITE MAN. You know the rules: stick to the story exactly as it happened.

BLACK MAN. Well, that's what was going through my mind.

WHITE MAN. But you didn't say a thing to him. All you did was sit there like a dunce and take his high-falutin bullshit like it was gospel.

BLACK MAN. He didn't know what I was thinking.

WHITE MAN. And he didn't care.

BLACK MAN. I'm only telling this story because I wanna prove all the shit I gotta put up with.

WHITE MAN. Then tell it like it is, man. Cut the crap about what you shoulda or coulda said.

BLACK MAN. Lemme tell you what I did say.

WHITE MAN. You said nothing!

BLACK MAN. I mean the next class.

WHITE MAN. No way.

BLACK MAN. Come on, man!

WHITE MAN. You had your turn.

BLACK MAN. It just take a second.

WHITE MAN. I ain't falling for that shit again.

BLACK MAN. What shit?

WHITE MAN. Last time I gave somebody a break, he didn't return the favor.

BLACK MAN. You still crying about that sorry-assed nigger beat you in that spelling bee? You just dissing me because he was black and I'm black, is that it?

WHITE MAN. (*Throws hands out in disgust.*) There you go with that because-I'm-black bullshit! Why you gotta resort to that?

(LIGHTS go out on him with the snap of the BLACK MAN's finger.)

BLACK MAN. Because it works. (*A beat.*) Like I was saying, the next class, the faggot started talking about how he's so against capital punishment.

(LIGHTS go up on WHITE MAN, back in character of professor.)

WHITE MAN. As the philosopher Albert Camus concludes in his essay "Reflections on the Guillotine": "There will be no lasting peace in the heart of individuals or in social customs until death is outlawed."

BLACK MAN. Yo, man.

WHITE MAN. Yes?

BLACK MAN. He ever live in the ghetto?

WHITE MAN. Excuse me?

BLACK MAN. Let him live in America before he say he against the death penalty. I'm tired a all these know-it-all writers talking jive from their safe little newsroom.

WHITE MAN. Are you a proponent of capital punishment?

BLACK MAN. Make no difference if I am or I ain't. I ain't making the rules. 'Cause if I did, there wouldn't be no more brothers walking home with one eye behind they backs worrying if some nigger's gonna cut them. There wouldn't be no crack dens next to my house. There wouldn't be no sisters hustling me the second I walk out my door. I'd kill them all.

WHITE MAN. Do you realize who would be the ones executed? Forty-two percent of black men in Washington, D.C. between the ages of eighteen and thirty-five are either on parole, in prison, awaiting trial, or being sought by the police. And many of these are for capital offenses.

BLACK MAN. So?

WHITE MAN. (*Incredulously.*) So? Young black males would be executed wholesale. It would be genocide.

BLACK MAN. Then if it makes you feel better, kill some a them corrupt white people while you at it.

WHITE MAN. I think you miss the point.

BLACK MAN. I think *you* miss the point. What you trying to do, stand in as the savior for the forty-two percent? Why ain't you worrying about the other fifty-eight percent? (*Gestures to fellow students.*) That's us. We ain't nothing to you?

WHITE MAN. Don't you feel any *identification* with the many incarcerated young African-American men who are victims of their environment?

BLACK MAN. You going crazy because I'm a black man with a different point of view than you expect. You want me to fall right in line with the rest of them niggers who say "right on" when you talk that jive.

WHITE MAN. I'm not suggesting that at all.

BLACK MAN. Oh yes you are. I say burn their asses. You kill somebody—whether you black or white or yellow—then you gonna die. You talk too much trash—especially if you a professor—then you gonna eat trash. (*A beat. To audience.*) Hey, what was the use of going back to that class anymore? I dropped it. And a little while later, I dropped outta college altogether. Got me this job with the City for a while. Purchasing for Health and Hospitals. (*Chuckles.*) All these white boys looking to sell me.

(*The WHITE MAN assumes the character of a salesman holding a brochure.*)

WHITE MAN. Sir, if you just take a moment from your hectic schedule to review our line of infection control products, I'm sure you'll seriously consider using them.

BLACK MAN. Yeah. I . . .

WHITE MAN. An astute individual such as yourself will notice that our prices are competitive.

BLACK MAN. Well I . . .

WHITE MAN. And these are not F.O.B.—plant prices! They're *delivered*.

BLACK MAN. Listen I . . .

WHITE MAN. So Mr. Silverman, please remember us when you place your next order.

BLACK MAN. I ain't Mr. Silverman.

WHITE MAN. No?

BLACK MAN. No. Mr. Silverman's my boss.

WHITE MAN. But I . . . you . . .

BLACK MAN. You didn't gimme a chance to speak.

WHITE MAN. I kinda figured with the name Silverman. Not that that can't happen. I know a Puerto Rican Reilly. I'm sorry.

BLACK MAN. That's alright. I know a black Goldberg myself.

WHITE MAN. I think it woulda been worse if at first sight I'd say, "You're not Mr. Silverman, are you?"

BLACK MAN. Why'd that be worse?

WHITE MAN. Well, you know.

BLACK MAN. No. I don't.

WHITE MAN. I wouldn't want you to think . . .

BLACK MAN. Think what?

WHITE MAN. You know. That I'm in some way . . .

BLACK MAN. Oh, the *R* word?

WHITE MAN. May I see Mr. Silverman?

BLACK MAN. Why would I think that?

WHITE MAN. Is he in?

BLACK MAN. Are you?

WHITE MAN. Because if he's not, I can just leave the brochure with you . . .

BLACK MAN. It never entered my mind . . .

WHITE MAN. And call him another time . . .

BLACK MAN. (*Points to his head.*) Until you planted it there.

WHITE MAN. After he's had a chance to review it.

BLACK MAN. (*Smiles.*) And now that it's there, I know.

WHITE MAN. Know what?

BLACK MAN. You're anti-Semitic.

(Pause. The WHITE MAN stands with his mouth agape. The BLACK MAN laughs at his joke, reaches out to take the brochure.)

BLACK MAN. Just kidding. I bet you thought I was gonna call you anti-black.

WHITE MAN. That wouldn't bother me. But anti-Semitic?

(The BLACK MAN stops laughing, stares fuming at the White Man.)

WHITE MAN. Just kidding.

(LIGHT dims on BLACK MAN as the WHITE MAN addresses the audience.)

WHITE MAN. When my old dog Pepper died, I wrapped him up in an old blanket, laid him on the front passenger seat of my car, and headed to the ASPCA about three miles down Morris Park Avenue. (*BLACK MAN, not expecting this monologue, wants to react, but WHITE MAN doesn't miss a beat.*) It was a cold winter day and I had the car windows up because my heater wasn't working. There was a lotta snow on the ground so I had to drive real slow. And with my luck, I got stuck at every traffic light. After a while Pepper started to smell real bad.

BLACK MAN. (*Suspiciously.*) Hey yo.

WHITE MAN. The whole car filled up with the stink of Pepper. It was awful. I started choking. By the time I was only a couple blocks away—on the bad side of Morris Park—I couldn't take it no more.

BLACK MAN. What's this all about?

WHITE MAN. So I cranked down the window, threw my head out and heaved in the winter air. No sooner do I stick my head out the window then a nigger comes outta nowhere and puts a knife to my neck.

(LIGHTS up on the BLACK MAN.)

BLACK MAN. You didn't say nothing about no stickup.
WHITE MAN. I lied.
BLACK MAN. Well I ain't listening.
WHITE MAN. *(Contemptuously.)* So the *brother* said . . . *(Pause. Looks at BLACK MAN who has his fingers stuck in his ears.)* "Get out the car, motherfucker." And if it wasn't for the fact that coming round the corner was a cop car, I woulda been a dead man. So he ran across the street into one a them condemned buildings. But not before he sliced my neck. *(WHITE MAN pulls down his collar and reveals a long scar.)* Cops didn't even see what was going on. That nigger coulda had a field day on me. So I sat there with all my money still in my wallet and blood squirting outta my neck all over the front seat. The stink of dead Pepper didn't phase me after that.
BLACK MAN. *(Removes fingers from his ears.)* You finished?
WHITE MAN. I haven't told the moral of the story yet.
BLACK MAN. Which is?
WHITE MAN. Next time you think there ain't no stench worse than death, you've forgotten the stench of life.
BLACK MAN. *(Fuming.)* Big shit.
WHITE MAN. Big shit, huh? That's all you can say. It's just against your grain to show outrage when a brother commits a crime.
BLACK MAN. You know that's not true.
WHITE MAN. You can't do it. Telling bullshit stories about wimpy sociology professors and dopey guineas on the corner and salesmen afraid of their own shadows.
BLACK MAN. Your spelling bee story weren't so hot either.
WHITE MAN. But not a word about throat-slashing niggers. Why is that?

BLACK MAN. Because they my neighbors, that's why! I see them every day. What you want me to do, spit in their eye? You see them neighbors of John Gotti bitching about him? Hell no! Why? Because they scared. So scared that they go out they way to say what a good ole boy he is. Shit! They end up doing his bidding for him till they ain't no different than him theyselves. They be on TV saying how good he be for the community but they ain't fooling nobody. You can see the scare in they eyes so bad that the screen blinds you. They ain't crazy for no killer, they just plain ole scared. I know what that's all about. Happen to me all the time where I come from. I see them crack dealers and I say, (*Bowing.*) "Morning, sir!" Every time a junkie throw a fit in my face, I step aside and say (*Bowing.*) "Excuse me." When a sister gets raped by a nigger, I just shake my head and say, "She shoulda knowed better than to be out late at night." And I just look the other way whenever a boy gets his head blowed off for a goddam leather jacket. So fuck your throat, Jim! (*A beat.*) I got this dream.

WHITE MAN. No dreams allowed!

BLACK MAN. We playing by new rules now.

WHITE MAN. Says who?

BLACK MAN. We already given up trying to talk to each other.

WHITE MAN. We're still standing here, aren't we?

BLACK MAN. I ain't telling you where to stand, but we ain't talking. We ain't got nothing left to say to each other. (*To audience.*) Here's my dream: It's about a mushroom and a marshmallow. M-U-S-H-R-O-O-M and M-A-R-S-H-M-A-L-L-O-W. (*Sneers at the White Man.*) One day all the whites on the east coast scared of them urban blacks gonna keep moving west. At the same time all them whites on the west coast gonna keep moving east 'cause of the unruly west coast blacks. Then they all gonna squash together somewhere in the middle of America like in a Kansas cornfield. But them blacks gonna keep pushing outward, all over America. Meanwhile all them whites gonna be fit so tight together—like a giant marshmallow. They won't be able to see nothing but their own sweet whiteness, but they be damned if they leave their marshmallow 'cause a that big black mushroom out there. So the marshmallows gonna start dissing each other 'cause they sick and tired of living on top of they own kind. Whites bitching 'bout how they wasn't left nothing by the blacks and taking it out on each other. Offing each other every chance they get. And somewhere out there in that big mushroom a bunch a fat cat blacks gonna go around wondering, "I just can't figure out them white folks. They don't improve themselves, they burn down their neighborhoods, and kill they own kind."

WHITE MAN. Know why that'll never happen?

BLACK MAN. It *has* happened. Read any history book.

WHITE MAN. 'Cause whites don't have an own kind.

BLACK MAN. They do in my dream.

WHITE MAN. Keep dreaming. That's all you ever do. Your mind is sick with hate because all you see is black and white. Meanwhile the Asians, the Arabs: they're all passing your sorry ass by.

BLACK MAN. Nobody's passing me by.

WHITE MAN. Like hell they ain't, you loser.

BLACK MAN. Watch what you saying now.

WHITE MAN. Watch what I'm saying? This is America, loser.

BLACK MAN. Look, man. I let you call me nigger and I didn't say shit when you talked about my junkie mother. But you ain't calling me a loser.

WHITE MAN. I called you a loser in court and I'm calling you a loser now.

BLACK MAN. I wasn't convicted.

WHITE MAN. But you killed her.

BLACK MAN. No I didn't.

WHITE MAN. There wasn't justice in that courtroom.

BLACK MAN. That's the same courtroom locks up half the niggers in The Bronx.

WHITE MAN. YOU KILLED MY SISTER!

BLACK MAN. It wasn't me, man.

WHITE MAN. YOU KILLED MY SISTER!

BLACK MAN. No I didn't.

WHITE MAN. YOU KILLED MY SISTER!

BLACK MAN. (*Bolts toward the White Man.*) I didn't kill your sister, but I'm a kill you.

(The WHITE MAN drops to his knees as the BLACK MAN stands over him with his clenched fists raised over his head.)

BLACK MAN. Get up!
WHITE MAN. (*Cowering.*) No.
BLACK MAN. I said up!
WHITE MAN. I can't.
BLACK MAN. Up!
WHITE MAN. I'm begging you.
BLACK MAN. Up, you motherfucker!
WHITE MAN. Can't you see I'm begging you for my life? MY SISTER DIDN'T BEG FOR HERS, BUT I'M BEGGING FOR MINE!
BLACK MAN. What you saying?
WHITE MAN. (*Sobbing, with each "I saw her" HE makes a stabbing motion.*) I saw her! You stabbed her before she even saw you!
BLACK MAN. (*Backs off in horror.*) You crazy.
WHITE MAN. I saw her! After you stabbed her a second time she punched you right in your face!
BLACK MAN. Wasn't me.
WHITE MAN. I saw her! She looked you dead in the eye and went for your arm!
BLACK MAN. No, man.
WHITE MAN. I saw her! But you stabbed her a fourth time. That's the only time I heard her: a soft groan. I saw her! Her arm swung wild but I could tell it was only a dead jerking. She was dead standing up.
BLACK MAN. Chill out, brother.
WHITE MAN. Then she dropped. But you weren't finished. You hit her a sixth (*Stabs the air.*) and a seventh time. (*Stabs the air. Pause. Strangely serene.*) I saw her.
BLACK MAN. But you didn't see me.
WHITE MAN. Yes I did.
BLACK MAN. It wasn't me, man.

WHITE MAN. My sister's dead.

BLACK MAN. I didn't kill your sister.

WHITE MAN. It was dark. I can't be sure.

BLACK MAN. Maybe somebody looked like me.

WHITE MAN. I think it was.

BLACK MAN. Think?

WHITE MAN. I don't know.

BLACK MAN. You didn't testify.

WHITE MAN. It wouldn't of made a difference.

BLACK MAN. And you . . .

WHITE MAN. Didn't do nothing to help her. I watched her die. (*A beat.*) This country is being driven crazy with fear.

BLACK MAN. That's enough, man.

WHITE MAN. I stood frozen in the shadows of my own house. I didn't know how to help her.

BLACK MAN. And I was falsely arrested, jailed, and put on trial.

WHITE MAN. (*Rises slowly.*) And then set free.

BLACK MAN. You a sick man. I thought you hated niggers 'cause you think you better than them. But now I see that ain't it at all. It's 'cause you hate yourself so much you can't see nothing any other way.

WHITE MAN. If it's sympathy you want, you won't find it here.

BLACK MAN. I ain't looking for your sympathy.

WHITE MAN. Then why're you here?

(THEY stare at each other, panting wildly.)

BLACK MAN. 'Cause this is where I live.

WHITE MAN. Is that why?

BLACK MAN. That's why.

WHITE MAN. Then move. Because I'm won't.

BLACK MAN. Now *that's* something that wouldn't make no difference.

WHITE MAN. Why?

BLACK MAN. I got nowhere to go. 'Cause from now on . . .

no matter what I do . . . no matter where I go . . . I'll always be the nigger that killed your sister. *(A beat. We can hear only their excited gasps.)* Am I right? *(With a brash rap tone, his pointing finger and his bopping body underscoring the syllables as the WHITE MAN turns his back to him.)* Look at me: What you scared of? Look at me: What you scared of? Look at me: What you scared of? Look at me: What you scared of?

(WHITE MAN collects himself. Turns to audience as the BLACK MAN continues to stare at him.)

WHITE MAN. Now let me tell you about my place in Perugia.
BLACK MAN. *(Sweetly, softly:)* Look at me: What you scared of?

(The WHITE MAN turns to the BLACK MAN, their eyes meeting for a brief moment.
LIGHTS dim to BLACK.)

END OF PLAY

COSTUME PLOT

WHITE MAN: Black trousers, black shirt, black socks, black leather shoes.

BLACK MAN: White jeans, white T-shirt, white socks, white sneakers.

PHILIP VASSALLO received a 1991 New Jersey State Council on the Arts playwriting fellowship for *Questions Asked of Dying Dreams*, four one-act plays which were produced in New Jersey (1992) and New York (1993). Philip's premiere New York production was his short play, "How You Get to Main Street?" (1993). His full-length plays, *The Mold of the Ring* (1992) and *Power Over Pain* (1993), were finalists in national play competitions, and his numerous essays on education, race relations, and the arts have appeared in various periodicals.

HIGHWIRE

by Brian James Shields

This play is dedicated to my family and friends for believing in me and to the Irish both here and abroad for inspiring me.
I wish you could have seen me Papa Jim.

Highwire was first presented on April 9, 1994 as part of the Nineteenth Annual Off-Off-Broadway Original Short Play Festival. With Jason O'Connell as Brendan, Al Pagano as Tim and Annette Previti as Katie. The play was directed by Phylis Ward Fox.

CHARACTERS

BRENDAN MOORE: Twenty-four-year-old native of Northern Ireland, he is in Manhattan illegally and works at the Black Rose Pub in Midtown. Slim hopes of legalization are harbored within him.

KATIE O'DONNEL: Twenty-two-year-old senior at Barnard College. She is in love with Brendan and wants to marry him for various reasons.

TIM SHANNON: Thirty-five-year-old New York City police officer and Irish American. He is a self-proclaimed patriot.

HIGHWIRE

The setting is Manhattan, present day in the Black Rose Pub. At stage right is the entrance and at stage left is the door to the bathrooms. Up left is an old jukebox. Scattered PATRONS are having a pint but action is frozen. LIGHTS are dim in the background, just enough to see the interior of the pub. SPOTLIGHT comes up center and we see BRENDAN MOORE. HE stands alone, smoking. As HE looks out over the audience BRENDAN begins his address through the smoke.

BRENDAN.
It was all right to fight back in nineteen sixteen
When the Post Office fell for the wearing of green
And the pub songs will sing of a more glorious time
But they've made being Irish in Ireland a crime

(Walks back to his place behind the bar. Action around him resumes and LIGHTS up, song continues on the juke. Enter TIM.)

BRENDAN. *(Friendlier tone than before.)* What'll be Tim?

TIM. A pint would do me right, it's getting cold out there. *(Gets his drink and sits down.)* Where's Katie tonight?

BRENDAN. She'll be by later, she's working on a paper or something.

TIM. Is that what she told you? *(Smiles and laughs at the standing joke.)* I've heard about those Barnard girls.

(BRENDAN pays him no heed as HE tends to wiping down the bar. TWO STRAGGLERS are left nursing their drinks and talking.)

BRENDAN. *(To the stragglers.)* Let's finish 'em up lads, those'll have to be the parting glass. I'd like to get home to my apartment.

TIM. Getting a bit possessive are you?

BRENDAN. I pay for my share of the rent. Besides it's only a temporary arrangement, you know that. (*Leans his elbows on the bar as TIM sits.*)

TIM. (*Mimicking his Northern brogue.*) Oh is it now?

BRENDAN. (*Looks at jukebox, annoyed.*) Time to unplug this. (*Walks over and back.*)

TIM. Hey, I like that song.

BRENDAN. You and the rest of the once-a-year Irish. If there was no seventeen in March, you'd never remember where the Hell you came from.

TIM. (*Offended by his bitterness.*) Listen Native Son, I'm damn proud and you know it. I bet you didn't read the paper today.

BRENDAN. No I didn't. Why?

TIM. Our boys got two more in Derry. Car bomb in front of a police barracks, of course no one's claimed responsibility. (*Laughs.*) But I'm sure we can guess who to thank.

BRENDAN. Look Tim, I'm a bit tired tonight. Could you spare me the lectures on patriotism?

TIM. Well, I just don't like to hear you criticizing the narrowbacks, some of us care more than you know. (*Under his breath.*) Some of us care more than you do.

BRENDAN. Don't take offense, I've just developed a disliking for the month since I've been here.

TIM. You might try not being so serious. What have you got to be mad about? So it's March. You're tips are probably better than they are around the fourth of July.

BRENDAN. There's some truth in that.

TIM. (*Finishes his pint and puts his coat on.*) Well, Mr. Moore. That's my thought for the evening. I best begin getting home. Some of us have to work in the morning.

BRENDAN. (*Laughs.*) New York's finest. Have a good night. Hey, where's your man Byrnes been lately?

TIM. He's been in Florida for a week with his family. He should be at work tomorrow. That reminds me, tomorrow night is our monthly meeting if you'd care to come.

BRENDAN. No, I can't. I'm taking Katie out to dinner tomorrow.

TIM. Sooner or later you're going to run out of excuses and you'll have to come. I guess until then I'll have to keep trying.

(A RAP is heard at the door and we see KATIE enter.)

TIM. Well good evening, Miss Kathleen.

KATIE. Hello yourself Timothy Shannon.

TIM. I'm off. Good night you two. Brendan, you might try and make it tomorrow night. I'm sure the boys would love to hear you talk. *(Pauses.)* It was just an idea. *(Exits.)*

BRENDAN. How are you, love? *(Leans over bar and meets her halfway, THEY kiss.)* I was starting to get worried, how late is that library open?

KATIE. All night, it's midterm season. *(Tries to kiss him again, gets his cheek.)* What was Tim talking about?

BRENDAN. Nothing, he's in his cups again.

KATIE. I bet I can guess. You've got more patriots in this pub.

BRENDAN. I know. It's the nature of the beast. Did you find the stuff I asked you for?

KATIE. *(Feigning hurt.)* Oh my day was fine thanks. My psych. midterm? Funny you should ask, I think I did really well. Which is strange considering the lack of sleep I went into it with. Of course you wouldn't know about that, you never snore loud enough to wake yourself up.

BRENDAN. I'm sorry, it's been on my mind all night. Your test went all right? *(SHE nods.)* Congratulations, I knew you'd do well. *(Back on task.)* So what did they say?

KATIE. I spoke to a really nice lady who told me that in a month or so they're going to be having an amnesty period. What they're going to do is run a lottery and pick a certain amount of people.

BRENDAN. *(Hopeful.)* No questions asked?

KATIE. They just need your name and place of birth. For reference purposes, you know.

BRENDAN. You mean for a background check. *(HE is*

disappointed.)

KATIE. Well of course, honey. They can't just let *anybody* in. It'd be like what happened with Cuba in the seventies. We have enough of our own criminals without having to send out for some. (*Sees his disappointment.*) Hey c'mon. Chin up, you've got a really good chance. I'm not saying it's a sure thing but it's better than nothing, right?

BRENDAN. Yeah, I'm sorry. You know I love you for this.

KATIE. Of course I know. Now can we go home or were you planning on sleeping here tonight?

BRENDAN. Well, the heat is better here. (*Smiles.*) All right, since you asked nicely I suppose I could see my way clear to letting you take me home. (*Comes around bar.*) But there'll be no shagging about, I'm a Catholic you know. (*Laughs and hugs her.*) Let's go, love.

(*KATIE heads out before Brendan and we hear TIM saying the line "Some of us care more than you do." SPOTLIGHT on BRENDAN, center stage.*)

BRENDAN.
I sit and I look through you
Your face goes ashen white
The shadow crawling cross my face
Is no trick of the light.
(*Looks up and straight out.*)
Bless me fa'er, it's been a long time.
Each man carries with him his own sin.
Let mine be that of omission.

(*Enter KATIE talking, THEY are outside in front of the pub.*)

KATIE. Honest to God, Brendan, I really don't understand you sometimes. You don't make any sense, you just don't.

BRENDAN. (*Quietly.*) Would you mind keeping your voice down? I'd rather not be the talk of the Rose if it's all the same to you.

KATIE. What is it with you? I swear to God you're like two different people at times.

BRENDAN. (*To himself.*) That's 'cause you only know one of us. (*To her.*) What would you like me to tell you?

KATIE. I can't even talk to you when you're like this. Thick headed micks! This is going nowhere, why is it every time I bring up commitment you get quiet? For Christ's sake Brendan, if I married you you'd be legit.

BRENDAN. Do you think that's why I'm with you? If you do then we might as well say our goodbyes now.

KATIE. I don't think that. If I did I wouldn't be here with you right now. Sometimes I feel like I'm trying harder to get you legalized than you are. Maybe I am. Selfishly I'm just sick of worrying and thinking to myself, "Is he coming home tonight?" I'm tired of it, Brendan.

BRENDAN. I'm sorry I didn't come with a guarantee, why don't you find yourself a nice American doctor. I hear they're very safe. (*HE is annoyed and defending himself.*)

KATIE. Fuck you then. I'm leaving. Why don't you go inside with your buddies and pine away for home.

BRENDAN. (*Realizing.*) Katie, please. I don't want you to go. It's just that now isn't a good time to discuss this. I'm trying to figure things out. Don't you see, you'll be out of school in May. I'm going to be here forever.

KATIE. There's no reason you can't leave here. You just need to get off your ass and take some steps yourself. I'm finished trying to help.

BRENDAN. Never mind, I'm sorry I brought it up.

KATIE. Don't do this. Can't we for once have a full argument without you backing away. You're like a little kid, peace at all costs.

BRENDAN. I just don't like to fight.

KATIE. Then don't fight me. Go down tomorrow and give them your place of birth and the other stuff they'll need. It's not that much they're asking for. I would think that if you love me as much as you say you do then you'd try and make sure they couldn't keep us apart. (*Puts her hand under his chin.*) Agreed?

BRENDAN. I'm not going to promise anything but I'll try.

KATIE. What are you so afraid of? (*Looks at her watch.*) Dammit, it's already three. I'm going home or I'll never be able to get up in the morning. Are you coming?

BRENDAN. I'll be along in a little while. Remember to lock the door, love. (*Enters the pub, SPOTLIGHT is on him and HE speaks.*)

Guess it's time to say goodbye now,
Go on Yankee break my heart,
There's no use looking toward tomorrow,
Guess we were finished from the start.

(*LIGHTS up and BRENDAN sits at a table doing the crossword. Enter TIM.*)

TIM. Good afternoon, lads. Hey Brendan, how are you today?

BRENDAN. I've been better, I've been worse. Yourself?

TIM. Doing very well. I see you got the paper. The north is on fire this week. It looks like an all out offensive. It does my heart good to read headlines like that. (*Laughs.*) I can tell you the boys in the club were a bit disappointed that you didn't show.

BRENDAN. I was busy. (*HE is not looking up from the paper but TIM sits anyway.*)

TIM. That's a damn shame, too busy for your countrymen. (*Lights a cigarette.*) Correct me if I'm wrong, but you weren't always that busy, now were you?

BRENDAN. (*Nervous laugh.*) Well, I sure as hell didn't have a job back in Ireland.

TIM. That's not what I'm talking about. I'm curious about your contacts back home.

BRENDAN. Do you think I'm James Bond here? I've relations in Ireland, not contacts.

TIM. Should I say comrades?

BRENDAN. Now you've got the wrong country. Look, Tim, I'm trying to do the crossword.

TIM. Brendan, I know why you're here. I've done my homework and I know what you've done. Do you take me for an idiot?

BRENDAN. I don't take you for anything.

TIM. Does Katie know?

BRENDAN. There's nothing to know. Shouldn't you be out arresting somebody or something like that. I understand this city is full of criminals. (*Smiles and goes back to his paper.*)

TIM. You know I could get you legalized. Katie told me about the lottery but you can't do that now can you? It seems to me your in a bad way.

BRENDAN. (*Looks up at him.*) I'm doing fine. What do you want, Tim?

TIM. How well do you remember Downpatrick during 1989?

BRENDAN. Probably not as well as you'd like me to.

TIM. I need names.

BRENDAN. If it's pen pals you're looking for, you might try the post office.

TIM. I'm not fooling around Brendan, I need your help and you need me to get your papers.

BRENDAN. I don't need anything.

TIM. There's nothing the Ulster Constabulary would like better than to see you make a homecoming appearance. I want names of who to contact over there. Some of the fellas from the Emerald Society want to make a contribution. A couple of bucks for the lads in the good fight.

BRENDAN. You've no fucking idea what it is you're talking about.

TIM. Hey man, I'm on your side. I want those English bastards out of our home as much as you do.

BRENDAN. You don't know anything. I can't help you.

TIM. There's no can about it. It'd be a damn shame if the wrong people knew you were working here. (*Condescending.*) Personally, I like you. But some of the boys really have their hearts set on this. You might end up serving your parting glass to Immigration.

BRENDAN. You treacherous bastard.

TIM. You've turned soft since you came here. You've forgotten the cause.

AN. And what do you know about the cause? What do
bout fucking Ireland except what you read in your little
ers? You sit there talking about "our home." It's my
fucking home and I wish to God I'd never seen the place. Do you
know what it's like there? Have you seen the lorries full of troops?
I've given it up, Tim. I'm done with it all. There's nothing worth
killing or dying for. (*Looks up at ceiling.*) I'm just starting to learn
that there are things worth living for.

TIM. That little rich girl'd drop you like the plague if she knew
what you'd done back in Ireland. We'll see how quick that Irish
charm wears off when she finds out you're a murderer. (*Smiles and
takes a drink.*) Don't be a fool I could have you legal in no time.

BRENDAN. And I'm supposed to trust you?

TIM. Hey c'mon I'm a cop. Besides I'm all you've got. Do you
doubt me, Brendan?

BRENDAN. You're a bastard. (*Glares at him.*)

TIM. I'm doing what you've become too weak to do anymore.
You're a damn disgrace and if I didn't know the good you'd done
I'd turn you in in a minute. You've forgotten the cause.

BRENDAN. (*Sadly.*) The glorious cause. You're blind. I don't
know how you sleep at night.

TIM. Let's not bring consciences into this lad, yours is blacker
than mine. I'm your last chance, now are you in or out? It'd be a
damn shame for little Katie to have to sleep alone.

*(Exit TIM. BRENDAN goes behind the bar. HE pours himself a
pint and starts to drink, LIGHTS dim and come back up.)*

KATIE. Jesus Christ, Brendan it's nearly five in the morning. I
got scared something had happened.

BRENDAN. (*Looking up.*) I'm all right. Just thinking.

KATIE. About last night

BRENDAN. I was wrong, I'm sorry.

KATIE. No it's not you at all. I've just never felt this way
before. I don't want to lose it. Or you. I love you.

BRENDAN. You shouldn't.

KATIE. (*Half joking.*) No, see Brendan the appropriate

response to that is I love you too. I thought we had worked on this.

BRENDAN. (*Sadly.*) Sorry.

KATIE. (*Realizing.*) Hey, I was just kidding. (*Comes behind him.*) What's wrong, honey.

BRENDAN. I don't belong here.

KATIE. Of course you belong here. This is going to be your new home. We shouldn't let anything stop us form getting you legal.

BRENDAN. Us?

KATIE. Yes, I was mad last night but I didn't mean everything I said. You know there's nothing I wouldn't do to help you.

BRENDAN. I don't belong here and I don't belong with you.

KATIE. You're drunk.

BRENDAN. I wish I was, love. (*Looks away.*)

KATIE. Tell me what it is. You're supposed to be able to tell me anything. Isn't that what this is all about. I mean, I love you. It would take a lot to change that. (*Reaches and touches his face.*) C'mon Brendan, please.

BRENDAN. I'm just tired, that's all.

KATIE. I'm not surprised. What were you and Tim sitting up talking about politics again? I honestly don't know why you bother, its not like you agree with anything he says, anyway. He's a nice guy but very ignorant about some things.

BRENDAN. I know. (*Lights a cigarette.*) He has this brilliant dream of the war in Ireland.

KATIE. Well are you surprised? He's a cop so he's obviously not opposed to violence like you are. To hear him talk you'd think he was from Downpatrick and you were from here. What was his topic of interest tonight? Has he figured a way to singlehandedly save the homeland? (*Smiles and shakes her head.*) I honestly don't know why you tolerate his company sometimes.

BRENDAN. We've all got our crosses to bear. He just doesn't know what he's talking about but he always wants to bring it up. The glorious struggle.

KATIE. Why don't you ever talk about it? Not that I mind, I was just curious.

BRENDAN. Some things are better left across the ocean.

KATIE. You know the first time I met you I asked one of the regulars what you were like. Do you know what he told me?

BRENDAN. (*Shakes his head.*) One of ours, I can't even imagine.

KATIE. (*Imitates his brogue.*) Watch yourself with that one. You'll not get much out of him, he's real good at keeping himself to himself.

BRENDAN. That's pretty good, have you been practicing?

KATIE. As a matter of fact I think it's probably from living with you. I was told the other day that I was starting to sound like you.

BRENDAN. Aren't you the lucky one? (*Looks at his watch.*) I think we should head home.

KATIE. (*Grabbing his arm.*) Not so fast, I want to know what's up. I played your game long enough, now out with it. What did Tim say that had you so upset?

BRENDAN. It's nothing, he's just a prick.

KATIE. Honey, he's always been a prick. Come on, really. I can tell something's up, it's all over your face.

BRENDAN. I've no wish to be analyzed.

KATIE. Too bad. Tell me.

BRENDAN. (*Motions to her.*) Come here. Katie, you know I love you. Do you at least know that?

KATIE. Of course I know. Brendan, what is it?

BRENDAN. (*Hugs her tightly.*) I'm scared, love.

KATIE. My God, what is it?

BRENDAN. Tim is involved in some things he's no business being involved with.

KATIE. Such as

BRENDAN. He's trying to run guns to Ireland.

KATIE. (*Shocked.*) But he's a cop. He told you this?

BRENDAN. He wants me to help. (*Lets go of her and takes a step back.*)

KATIE. Well you just tell him no. You don't have his hate. I can't believe he had the nerve to even ask you. Doesn't he know how you feel?

BRENDAN. I told him yes.

KATIE.You did what?

BRENDAN. He said if I helped him he'd get me my papers.

KATIE. And if you said no?

BRENDAN. I couldn't say no. (*Pauses.*) Katie, why do you think I came here?

KATIE. What do you mean why? You told me, there's no work over there and you couldn't stand living in the middle of a fight.

BRENDAN. (*With difficulty.*) Katie, I was—back home. Jesus, this is so hard. (*Looks down at the floor.*)

KATIE. (*Frightened.*) Tell me. Please.

(*SHE moves toward him and HE backs away.*)

BRENDAN. For a long time it was my fight. I didn't want to tell you but he knows the things I've done.

KATIE. But I thought you hated the violence over there.

BRENDAN. Don't you understand? It's like when you're raised in a battlefield you can't help but grow up like a soldier. I was throwing rocks at the lorries by the time I was seven. That's why I came here. I couldn't take it anymore. Being scared all the time, always reaching for a gun when some one knocked at the door. It got so that I was afraid of my own shadow. I would have died if I hadn't turned my back on it.

KATIE. (*With contempt.*) You were one of them. And now you're back with them.

BRENDAN. Love, I've nowhere to turn.

KATIE. Run away from here. Go to Boston or Philadelphia.

BRENDAN. I can't leave you, Katie. I love you too much to go. If I leave now I'll be running my whole life. When does this all stop?

KATIE. So you're going through with it.

BRENDAN. Do I have a choice? I can finally start over. Just this once and I'll be free and clear.

KATIE. Do you really believe that?

BRENDAN. I've come here to get away from it not re-enlist. For the first time in my life I don't feel dead inside when I get up in the morning. I don't ever want to feel like I did again. I swear to

God I'm telling you the truth.

KATIE. Can you live with yourself?

BRENDAN. (*Moving towards her.*) I'm doing this for you as much as I am for me. We can start a new life together. I love you, Katie.

KATIE. Brendan, I love you too. I just wish—

BRENDAN. There's no room for wishing here, love. Everything has come to a push and I've got to do this now. Do you think I'm going to like this?

KATIE. No but—

BRENDAN. I need you to stand by me. (*Hugs her.*) It'll be all right, you have to believe that. (*To himself.*) I have to believe that. (*To her again.*) This may be the land of opportunities but everything has its price. I'm learning that. It'll be all right.

KATIE. God help you, Brendan Moore.

(Dim LIGHTS and BRENDAN now stands center stage, at stage right is KATIE and at stage left is TIM. SPOT will shift from character to character as each speaks.)

BRENDAN. It was November, almost dark and the R.U.C. was making their last rounds before the change of shift. I was with Ferghal and Tommy Cahill. It had been a rough night and we were scared. At least I was. I had been sitting behind one of the spires of St. Bridget's watching for Tommy's signal. There was two of them and they were walking down towards where I was. There was a few other people in the street heading home but they weren't to be noticed. We were told they weren't important. Ferghal was on the roof across from me and he fired too early, he'd been drinking. They fired up at him and I fired back without looking. (*Pauses.*) I looked down and saw Tommy running and I looked to see where the soldiers were. They were both kneeling on the street. I thought to myself I must have gotten 'em both. Then I heard a woman scream and I saw something small lying still. I had killed her child.

TIM. (*Shouting, almost triumphantly.*) UP A LONG LADDER AND DOWN SHORT ROPE, TO HELL WITH KING BILLY AND GOD BLESS THE POPE AND IF THAT DOESN'T DO

THEN WE'LL TEAR HIM IN TWO AND SEND HIM TO HELL
WITH HIS RED, WHITE AND BLUE.

BRENDAN. We were told they weren't important. She was
seven years old.

TIM. (*Sings defiantly.*) A Nation once again, a Nation once
again, and Ireland long a province be a Nation once again.[1]

KATIE. An eye for and eye makes the whole world blind.

BRENDAN. Health and long life to you, The woman of your
choice to you, A child every year to you, Land without rent to you,
And may you die in Ireland.

TIM. By any means necessary.

KATIE. Do unto others as you would have done to you.

BRENDAN. I was scared. Our Father who art in Heaven
hallowed be thy name, another few feet and they're in my sight—
thy Kingdom come thy will be done on earth as it is in Heaven—
the sniper raised his rifle at first light and fired—Give us this day
our daily bread

*(TIM and KATIE will genuflect themselves as THEY repeat "A
Terrible Beauty is Born.")*

BRENDAN. And forgive us our trespasses—My God what
have I done—as we forgive those who trespass against us—And
lead us not into temptation but deliver us from evil.Amen.

(SPOTLIGHT out on TIM and KATIE.)

BRENDAN. But deliver us from evil. Amen. (*Pauses and then
genuflects.*) A terrible beauty is born.

(BLACKOUT as we hear a patriotic song played.)

END OF PLAY

---

[1] *A Nation Once Again* by Thomas Osborne Davis

COSTUMES

BRENDAN: Button down shirt tucked into blue jeans, white T-shirt underneath. Bucks or work boots; white apron folded over, tied around waist.

KATHLEEN: Tailored black pants with pleats and a nice blouse; winter coat, in an olive green (mid-calf length); black flats and a purse.

TIM: A dressed down suit; khaki slacks, a white shirt with a tie that can be loosened on stage; blue jacket and basic brown shoes.

PROPERTY PLOT

1 Bar and "Bar Back" with items such as: Guinness Stout, Bushmills Irish Whiskey, Jameson's Irish Whiskey, other assorted alcohols. Bar should be littered with ashtrays, coasters, pint glasses, bottles, rags etc. (u.s.l.)
1 round bar table, 3 chairs. On the table should be an ashtray and coasters. (d.s.r.)
3 bar stools.
2 newspapers—one is the *Irish Voice*, the other is the *New York Post*, opened to the crossword.
1 book bag—Kathleen.
2 packs of cigarettes— Brendan and Tim.
1 Zippo lighter—Tim.
1 service revolver, shoulder holster— Tim.

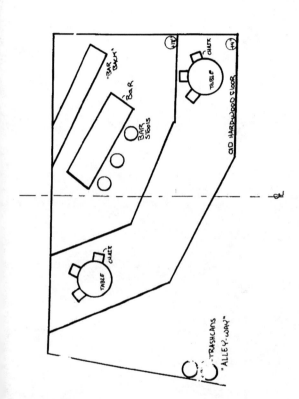

SCENE DESIGN
"**HIGHWIRE**"
SHELLI ADERMAN
3/8" = 1'-0"

PIZZA: A LOVE STORY

by Julianne Bernstein

Pizza: A Love Story was presented by Extra Cheese Productions for the Nineteenth Annual Short Play Festival on April 7, 1994 under the direction of Laurie Wessely, with the following cast:

JANET...Lisa DeBenedetti

JEFFREY ....Sean Baldwin

RITA..Amie Bermowitz

RICK ....Gregory Northrop

OFFICER ....Garth Kravits

(Above actors are members of Actors' Equity Assocation)

Pizza: A Love Story was originally presented at the Walnut Street Theater in Philadelphia as part of the Lunchtime Theater Series. It was directed by Mark Cofta.

Special thanks: Marlene and Jeff Baldwin,
Marie Adamo, John Dough's Pizza,
Pizza Plus, John Porter

CHARACTERS

JANET – Mid-to-late twenties. The Mary Tyler Moore type. Steady and stable, but frenetic and volatile in the face of danger.

JEFFREY – Mid-to-late twenties. A yuppie with a good sense of humor and values. A little weak-kneed, but nothing a good woman can't fix.

RICK – Age 24, delivers pizza. Understated, yet filled with good advice and a loyalty to the pizza industry.

RITA – Age 30, Janet's sister. Loud, boisterous. She has been through a lot, and isn't afraid to explore further.

POLICE OFFICER – Late twenties. Interested in keeping crime off the streets, as long as he can do it from his squad car and does not have to get out. Always eating.

TIME & PLACE

The present. A bachelor's apartment.

To Michael D'Anna,
who brought out the "extra cheese" in all of us.

PIZZA: A LOVE STORY

Scene: Jeffrey's apartment. 10:00 p.m. A cold winter evening.

It is spare but very nice with a desk, a sofa, coffee table, and small one-man bar. Things are slightly unkempt—a couple of magazines on the floor, a raincoat slung across a chair. A bachelor's pad that needs a woman's touch. JEFFREY and JANET enter. JEFFREY takes off his overcoat and scarf and drops it onto the sofa. He has just begun the process of trying to get a stain out of his shirt—going over to the bar, wetting a paper towel, and rubbing it into his shirt. JANET follows him in.

JEFFREY. Right. I know. I'll get a . . .

JANET. . . . a napkin . . .

JEFFREY. . . . dabbed with . . .

JANET. . . . vinegar.

JEFFREY. Yes, yes, yes, yes.

JANET. *(Taking off her coat.)* All Italian sauces are oil-based. Oil, Jeffrey. You need to get it before it settles. Before the material absorbs it. I mean, once it settles . . . the oil, I mean . . .

JEFFREY. Right. I'll take it . . .

JANET. . . . off and get it over to the dry cleaners right away. The dry cleaners. Jeffrey. *(Pause.)* I'm sorry. It's your shirt. It's your stain. What do I know?

JEFFREY. *(Smiling.)* You do know. Stop that. You know stains.

JANET. *(Goes to the closet to hang up her coat. There are no hangers.)* Jeffrey, where are your . . .

JEFFREY. . . . hangers. They're in the closet. In the bedroom.

JANET. *(Starts to exit into the bedroom. SHE grabs his overcoat and scarf from off the sofa.)* Give me your jacket. I'll take it inside.

(HE takes off his jacket and hands it to her. SHE exits into the bedroom.)

JEFFREY. Wait!

(JANET turns around.)

JEFFREY. Uh . . . I'm cold.
JANET. I'll get you a sweatshirt.
JEFFREY. No. My jacket. Please?

(SHE hands him his jacket and exits into the bedroom. HE takes out a ring box from his shirt pocket. HE puts it in his shirt pocket but it sticks out like a miniature breast.)

JANET. *(Entering, still carrying the coats.)* Jeffrey!
JEFFREY. Yes, honey? *(HE quickly folds his arms across his chest.)*
JANET. They're all being used right now. What should I do?
JEFFREY. I don't know what to tell you, babe.

(SHE looks at him begrudgingly and exits. HE pulls the ring from his shirt pocket, and finally puts the ring in the desk drawer.)

JANET. *(Entering, and picking up magazines off the floor.)* You need hangers.
JEFFREY. *(Taking her by the shoulders.)* Tomorrow. You'll come with me. Together, we'll go shopping for hangers.
JANET. How romantic. *(SHE is about to toss the magazines into the wastebasket.)*
JEFFREY. Hey! Give me that.
JANET. *(Reading.)* "Are you truly the romantic type or are you just making a useless attempt? Rate yourself."
JEFFREY. Janet!
JANET. How'd you do? Did you pass?
JEFFREY. Give it here.

(*HE tries to grab the magazine from her, SHE runs around the room with it.*)

JANET. (*Reading.*) "Number one."

JEFFREY. Don't you dare.

JANET. C'mon. Just one.

JEFFREY. It's only for men.

JANET. "How would you present your fiance with an engagement ring?"

JEFFREY. I beg you, please. Enough.

JANET. "A: Play 'treasure hunt' and make her look for it." (*Looking up.*) That's awful. Who wants to look for their own present?

JEFFREY. Give it back. I failed. O.K.?

JANET. (*Hands him the magazine.*) Dinner was wonderful.

JEFFREY. Dinner was wrong. Are you kidding? I asked for candlelight, I asked for music. I didn't ask for Christmas bulbs and—ugh! Those obnoxious—what the hell were they anyway? Elks or Buffalos?

JANET. Oh, they were fun. Those cute hats. And that song.

JEFFREY. Janet, I couldn't hear myself think. I couldn't hear what you were thinking.

JANET. What I was thinking?

JEFFREY. I can do that.

JANET. Hear what I'm . . .

JEFFREY. . . . thinking.

JANET. Know . . .

JEFFREY. . . . what you're thinking.

JANET. *That's* romantic.

JEFFREY. What?

JANET. That was a romantic thing . . . you just said.

JEFFREY. Great. A hundred and fifty-bucks later and *now* I get to the good stuff. Some anniversary.

JANET. Are you sure it's our anniversary?

JEFFREY. Oh no. Not again.

JANET. But was it really a "date"?

(HE swings his legs up on the couch and tries to lie back. SHE knocks them off, and sits down.)

JANET. We went shopping for a new litter box for my cat. That's not very exciting.

JEFFREY. Oh, I don't know. I got excited . . . when Chester was trying out his new box . . . and christened it with his first turd.

JANET. Jeffrey, that's gross!

(JANET grabs the rolled up magazine from JEFFREY and hits him with it. THEY play—saying things like "You're the turd." and "Meow, meow." THEY tickle each other until HE is lying on his back, and SHE is on top of him.)

JEFFREY. Janet, there's something I—

JANET. Oooh, your shirt. It's sticky. Go. Vinegar.

JEFFREY. Vinegar?

JANET. I read something somewhere about vinegar.

JEFFREY. It's just that I . . . just . . . something I want to ask you.

JANET. O.K. Hurry, then.

(HE smiles and exits.

SHE kicks off her shoes so she can get down to the nitty gritty of cleaning—pulling out a various assortment of items from underneath the sofa—clips, pens, crumpled pieces of paper, socks, underwear, spoons, a couple of paperback novels, etc. SHE places the books back on the bookshelf, the spoons over to the bar, the socks and underwear in the trash. SHE picks up all the pens and paperclips and brings them over to the desk. SHE opens the desk drawer and throws the pens and clips in. SHE shuts it. SHE stops, SHE opens it, takes out the ring box, and opens it. SHE screams joyfully.)

JEFFREY. *(Entering, carrying his shirt.)* What? What is it?

JANET. *(Hiding the ring under her arm.)* Nothing.

JEFFREY. Why'd you scream like that?
JANET. Jeffrey! Go put on a shirt!
JEFFREY. But—
JANET. *(Covering her eyes.)* Jeffrey!

(HE exits. SHE quickly puts the ring on and screams a silent scream. SHE takes it off and puts it back in the desk drawer and sits on the couch, calmly, peacefully, with her hands folded on her lap.)

JANET. Honey?
JEFFREY. *(From the bedroom.)* Yeah, honey?
JANET. Are you coming?
JEFFREY. Sure.
JANET. Hurry.
JEFFREY. We've got all night, sweetie.
JANET. All night. Yes.
JEFFREY. All day tomorrow, too. If you'd like.
JANET. All day?
JEFFREY. Right. All day.
JANET. All . . . *(To herself.)* Yes. All day tomorrow. All day. Every day. For the rest of my . . . *(A flush of anxiety comes over her. SHE starts breathing heavily. SHE falls forward with her head between her knees. SHE runs out—no shoes, no coat—SHE runs back in. Freezing. SHE goes over to the phone, picks it up and dials.)* Rita? Hey, it's me. *(Pause.)* I'm at Jeffrey's. I need you. I need you. I need you. *(Pause.)* Please. I need your advice. About Jeffrey. He's going to ask me to marry him, Rita. Marry him. *(Pause.)* So? So? I love him but I can't say "yes." I can't say "no"—I don't want to lose him. *(Pause.)* Come over. Please. I need you here. I need to talk to you. *(Pause.)* I don't know what he's got in his refrigerator. *(Pause.)* There will be food, I promise. *(Pause.)* Pizza? Yes . . . extra pepperoni, extra cheese . . . Now get over here. NOW!

(SHE hangs up the phone. JEFFREY enters. HE goes to her; HE touches her face and then her hands.)

JEFFREY. Your hands are cold.

JANET. Yeah, well.

JEFFREY. Come here. I'll warm them for you.

(HE leads her to the couch. THEY sit. SHE reaches out for the papers and things on the coffee table; HE takes her hands back; SHE reaches out again.)

JEFFREY. Janet, give me your hand.

JANET. No.

JEFFREY. Give me your hand.

JANET. No.

JEFFREY. All I want is your hand, damnit!

JANET. *(Reaching under the couch and then crawling around it.)* Have you looked under here lately? It's like there's other life. Whole civilizations, cultures—

JEFFREY. *(Laughing.)* How about that? As we've been making out, life as we don't know it, has been going on right under our very kissy, kissy noses.

JANET. There must be two thousand paper clips under here.

JEFFREY. Darling—

JANET. Three hundred pens.

JEFFREY. Sweetie—

JANET. Some kind of fruit pit.

JEFFREY. Bunny rabbit.

JANET. And dustballs—everywhere!

JEFFREY. Janet, what's the matter with you?

(SHE reaches out and starts to fiddle with the small pieces of paper SHE pulled from underneath the sofa that are now in front of her on the coffee table.)

JANET. Honey, it's just that I don't want . . . I don't know . . . I'm not ready . . . it's all so . . . honestly . . . I have a hard time . . . letting an opportunity like this go by, but . . .

JEFFREY. What is it?

JANET. *(Reading.)* AN EXTRA LARGE PIZZA, CHOICE OF TWO TOPPINGS, TWO LARGE COKES, ALL FOR UNDER TWENTY-ONE FIFTY AND DELIVERED IN LESS THAN FIVE MINUTES! THIS IS PERFECT!!! *(SHE goes over to the phone and dials. Into the phone.)* Hi. *(Pause.)* Yeah. I'd like two large ones. I've got this coupon and it says an extra large, two toppings, two—How quick can you get here? *(Pause.)* Uh . . . nix the toppings. Make it plain and forget the ice. Pour the cokes and come on over. 444 Stevens Way. Right. Come swiftly. Gallop a pace you fiery footed steeds. *(Pause.)* Oh. Shakespeare. *(Pause.)* *Romeo and Juliet. (Pause.)* Oh. Well, at that point, Juliet's waiting for the Nurse to come back with news of Romeo . . . she's impatient. So, hurry up. For the sake of Juliet—for the sake of art—roll that dough, spread that sauce, pop it in, and I can't wait. Hurry!

(SHE hangs up. SHE looks at JEFFREY who is sitting on the couch, stunned.)

JEFFREY. You want a pizza?
JANET. Don't you?
JEFFREY. Not after a four course Italian dinner and spumoni for dessert.
JANET. I'm starving. I gotta have a pizza. I ordered one. And that's that.

(JEFFREY laughs.)

JANET. What? What's so funny?
JEFFREY. *(Laughing.)* You know, I love what you do to this place.
JANET. What? What I do?
JEFFREY. Even though it's crazy. I trust you that there's some logic behind all this pizza behavior. And that it'll lead us . . . both . . . in the right direction.
JANET. *You? You* need direction?
JEFFREY. Yes.

JANET. But—"Shampoo. Rinse. Repeat." That's you. You write those directions. You create them.

JEFFREY. I know, but—

JANET. And you're the best, too. I was in the supermarket today and people were complimenting you on your work—you know, that last job you did.

JEFFREY. *Lady Dry?*

JANET. That's it. "Turn dial to raise product. Do not apply to broken skin. Lift arm." Good work. Jeffrey. Wonderful work. WHERE'S THAT PIZZA!!!

JEFFREY. Janet, try and relax.

JANET. Right. Getting all worried and anxious isn't going to make that pizza get here any faster. No, sir. It's in God's hands, now. It's up to him. It's out of our control.

JEFFREY. Shhh. *(Putting his arms around her waist.)* Now. Tonight. *(Kissing her neck.)* One year ago—give or take a week or so—we met, we had our "first date," we kissed . . . How do you feel?

JANET. Tense. Really, really tense.

JEFFREY. Oh. Here. *(HE leads her over to the sofa, and sits her down. HE rubs her shoulders, back, and neck area.)* There. Now, close your eyes.

JANET. How will being blind relieve me of my tension?

JEFFREY. Shhh, Janet, I—

JANET. Agh! *(SHE stands up.)*

JEFFREY. What's wrong?

JANET. It's all that dust. I think I'm allergic. I'm having a chemical reaction. I gotta sit down. *(SHE sits.)*

JEFFREY. Wait.

(HE moves towards the desk. As soon as HE is about to retrieve the ring, SHE screams again.)

JANET. Agh! *(SHE stands up.)*

JEFFREY. What, now?

JANET. It's the sitting down—the getting up. The sitting up—the getting down again. That's why I'm dizzy. Light-headed.

Light-footed. Feet. Feet. That's it! Yeah. My feet. My shoes. Where are my shoes? (*SHE searches around for her shoes and finds them where SHE kicked them off before. SHE puts them on.*) There. Take me home now.

    JEFFREY. But I haven't asked you yet. I want to ask you to—

    JANET. My coat! Where's my coat. The bedroom.

(*SHE starts to exit towards the bedroom. JEFFREY pulls her back.*)

    JEFFREY. Sit down.

(*SHE sits but buries her head in the couch, cowering in fear.*)

    JEFFREY. Sit up.

(*SHE sits up and looks away.*)

    JEFFREY. Look at me.

    JANET. *(Looking straight at him.)* I love our life, Jeffrey.

    JEFFREY. What?!!

    JANET. I love our life together. As it is—I mean—the way you can just sit *there,* and I can stand *here.* And you can sit *there,* and I can pick up the phone *here.* (*SHE does so.*) And you can sit *there,* and I can order a pizza . . . *here.* And you can sit *there* and I can hang up the phone, here. (*SHE does so.*)—and you can sit there and I can—

    JEFFREY. Forget it. (*HE crosses upstage.*)

    JANET. Now, where are you going?

(*HE then puts on a classic romantic tune from the "Greatest Hits" collection of a popular crooner.*)

    JANET. His "Greatest Hits," I take it?

    JEFFREY. *(Extending his hand and gently pulling her up.)* Shut up and dance with me.

    JANET. But you know how I get. My legs turn to jelly and my

heart starts to flutter.

JEFFREY. So what?

JANET. I DON'T WISH TO HAVE JELLY LEGS OR GET GOD-DAMN HEART FAILURE!

(JEFFREY releases her. THEY both sit. HE looks at her, takes a deep breath.)

JEFFREY. Janet, I want to dance with you the rest of my life.

JANET. Do you mean like "forever"? Like we couldn't stop dancing even if we *wanted* to? You know, like in the movie with Jane Fonda about people dancing and horses dying.

JEFFREY. *(Pause.)* Wait here. *(HE starts to exit.)*

JANET. Where are you going?

JEFFREY. To boil rice.

JANET. Rice?

JEFFREY. You feed it to me when I'm acting up.

JANET. Well . . . great. Please. Yes. Rice. Yes. And don't forget. You have to watch it or it'll boil over. You have to sit and watch it.

JEFFREY. Fine. I'll go . . .

JANET. —boil . . .

JEFFREY. —the rice.

JANET. Thank you.

JEFFREY. YOUR WELCOME!!!

(HE exits. SHE picks up the phone and dials.)

JANET. *(To herself.)* Rita, where are you? Good. Good. You're on your way. *(SHE hangs up and dials again. Into the phone.)* 9-1-1!!? I wanted 900. Get some advice, you know? *(Pause.)* Don't go. Uh . . . uh . . . my emergency? Well, yes. I'm here with someone who's . . . about to jump. Yeah. Well, "suicide" is a really strong word. It's more like "having a fit." Well, no. More like "on the edge." No. More like "over the edge." *(Pause.)* Could you? Good. 444 Stevens Way. Hurry. Right. *(SHE hangs up.)*

JEFFREY. *(Enters.)* Who were you talking to?

JANET. I don't know.

JEFFREY. What do you mean, you don't know?

JANET. I picked up the phone. I dialed a number. Some numbers. And then, I don't know. Someone answered. And I started thinking about when I was a kid—how my sister and I—we used to fight when my grandmother called up. Both of us wanted to talk to her first—and we'd fight and fight over the phone, until my grandmother hung up—she'd just hang up. Can you imagine—your own grandmother hanging up on you? Huh? Where's my rice?

JEFFREY. It's cooking.

JANET. But you have to watch it. You can't leave the rice.

JEFFREY. I put it on low. Listen, I was sitting there staring at the rice . . . on low. And I thought to myself. I'm just like that rice—I'm living my life on low. Just waiting for something to happen. But *I've* got to make it happen. And before the pizza gets here.

(DOORBELL rings.)

JANET. And here it is. Yeah! *(SHE opens the door. It's RITA.)*

JEFFREY. Rita?

JANET. Yes. You didn't think we could eat all that pizza by ourselves, did you?

JEFFREY. I didn't plan on Rita coming over.

RITA. Oh, she can't see me. Her sister, her only sister, unless you can fit her into *your* schedule. I'm here because my sister is my blood. She called. I cared. I came. Where's the pizza?

(The DOORBELL rings again. JANET goes to open it. It is RICK.)

RICK. Pizza.

JEFFREY. Come in. They're getting cold.

RICK. Don't worry about your pizzas, ma'am. Because no matter how cold it gets out there, your pizzas stay fresh and hot in these insulated carriers.

JEFFREY. How much?

RICK. Eighteen dollars fifty cents, sir.

RITA. *(To Rick.)* I'll take that.

(SHE tries to take one of the pizzas. RICK holds onto them for dear life.)

RITA. Do we have a problem here?

RICK. Rule: Don't let the pizzas leave you until exchange of currency has occurred.

RITA. Excuse me, sir, but—

RICK. No. I'm no "sir", ma'am. I'm Rick. Not the Rick. Just Rick.

JEFFREY. Hang on. My wallet's in the bedroom. My other pants.

JANET. No, Jeffrey. No way. I ordered the pizza. I'll pay.

JEFFREY. O.K. then, where's your purse, Janet? Let's pay for the pizza.

JANET. Hmm. My purse. My purse. Where is my purse?

RICK. Where'd you put it?

JANET. I can't remember.

RICK. The bedroom?

RITA. How do you know?

RICK. I'm used to this.

JEFFREY. I'm going into the bedroom. I'm getting the purse. *(HE exits.)*

RITA. *(Referring to the pizzas.)* You can put those down.

RICK. Can't. Rule: Don't let the pizzas leave you until exchange of currency has occurred.

(RITA glares at him.)

JEFFREY'S VOICE. *(From the bedroom.)* Where is it?!!

JANET. Look on the bed. Look all around. Look in the dresser. In every drawer. On the pillows. In the pillows . . .

RICK. "What light through yonder window breaks."

RITA. Excuse me?

RICK. "Arise, fair sun, and kill the envious moon." I can't

believe it. It all came back to me on the way over here. And I didn't even do Romeo. I handed Mercutio his sword for the big fight, and made sure the poison was all set up for the big swallow. Romeo was my best friend. And you know what? Underneath his Romeo costume, he was wearing the coolest-looking Grateful Dead T-shirt you ever saw. Only he and I knew he was wearing it. "Arise, fair sun, and kill the envious moon." Wow. (*HE points to Janet's purse at the foot of the couch.*)

RICK. Hey! There! What light!

(*JANET grabs it.*)

JEFFREY'S VOICE. (*From the bedroom.*) I can't find it anywhere.

(*SHE unzips the front of Rick's jacket and stashes the purse inside.*)

RICK. Hey!
JANET. I need your help. Both of you. Don't leave me.
RICK. I am a messenger. I have wings!
RITA. I gotta eat. I'm not goin' anywhere.

(*JANET steps back. JEFFREY enters.*)

JEFFREY. It's not there.

(*RICK gestures towards JANET that HE itches and the purse is sitting in an uncomfortable position.*)

JEFFREY. (*To Rick.*) You got a problem?

(*RICK pulls out the purse from his jacket and hands it to JANET.*)

JANET. Just a little game to pass the time.

(*ALL THREE laugh uncomfortably.*)

JEFFREY. Never mind. Please pay the boy. His hands are probably burning up from those god-damn pizzas.

RICK. I'm not a boy, sir. I'm twenty-five years old. And don't worry, because with these insulated pizza jackets—

JEFFREY. ALRIGHT! *(Pause.)* Janet, pay him.

JANET. *(Pulls out her wallet.)* Oh my God. What an awful shame. I have no cash. None at all. I feel like such a fool.

RICK. "And none but fools do wear it; cast it off." It's all coming back to me. And I didn't even do Romeo!

JEFFREY. *(To Rick.)* Take the pizzas back.

RITA. No, don't.

JEFFREY. I said, take 'em back.

JANET. But what about the money?

RICK. It'll come out of my pocket.

JANET. You can't let that happen, Rick. Your self-respect. Your integrity.

RICK. You're right. Jeff, I gotta have my money.

RITA. A check. A check. Write him a check.

RICK. No can do. No can do.

JEFFREY. Why not? For God's sake, why not . . . Rick?

RICK. The last one bounced. Bing-bong-boing. The boss was pissed. Real pissed. It came out of my tips and more. No more checks. No more checks.

JEFFREY. Call your boss. I want to talk to him.

RICK. Do you know Rick?

JEFFREY. Rick? There's *another* Rick?

RICK. My boss. Rick. He's not *the* Rick. He's just Rick. My Boss. Rick. Do you know him?

JEFFREY. Never met the man.

RICK. Are you like looking for a job? 'Cause he's not hiring now.

JANET. You know, honey, if you're interested, why *not* call Rick's boss? Even if he isn't hiring *now*, let him keep you in mind for a position later on.

JEFFREY. I DO NOT WANT TO WORK FOR RICK'S PIZZA. DO YOU HEAR ME? I AM NOT EVEN REMOTELY

INTERESTED IN HOW RICK IS GETTING ALONG OR WHAT
HE THINKS. I ONLY WANT TO SEE IF WE CAN PAY FOR
THE PIZZAS WITH A CHECK!

(Silence.)

    RITA. It's our only hope. Please. Let's ask.
    JEFFREY. *(To Rick.)* You. Over here.

*(RICK crosses to Jeffrey at the desk. JEFFREY picks up the phone,
turns RICK around, reads the phone number off of his jacket
and dials.)*

    JEFFREY. Yeah. Hi. Hang on. We've got your boy here with a
couple of extra large ones. Here he is. *(JEFFREY puts the phone to
Rick's ear.)*
    RICK. They want to write a check. *(Pause.)* Yes, sir. Yes, sir.
O.K., sir. Thank you, sir. Yes, sir. I'll be right there. Yes, sir. I'll
tell them.
    JEFFREY. *(Takes the phone from Rick's ear and hangs it
up).*Well?
    RICK. It's either your cash or my butt.
    JEFFREY. Well?
    JANET. We can't let Rick have Rick's butt.
    RICK. Yeah!
    RITA. Yeah!
    JANET. Yeah!
    JEFFREY. That does it! *(HE exits into the bedroom.)*
    RICK. Nice place you got here.
    JANET. It's his.
    RICK. So you guys live in separate houses?
    JANET. Yeah.
    RICK. Good thing.
    JEFFREY. *(Entering, wearing his overcoat and scarf.)* I left my
wallet in the car. Sit tight. Cash is on its way.
    RITA. Hurry!

(JEFFREY exits.)

RITA. Is there *anything* to eat?

JANET. Rita, Rita, tell me what to do.

RITA. No chow, no chat. That's our pact.

RICK. Anything I can do to help?

RITA. Hand over a slice of cheese.

RICK. No way.

RITA. Janet.

JANET. In the kitchen. Organic chips. Top shelf. Next to the
the sun-dried tomatoes.

(RITA exits.)

RICK. Do you have a copy of that play around here?

JANET. What? *Romeo and Juliet*? Well, I don't know. Let me
see. *(SHE goes over to the bookshelf and browses through books.)*
Here.

(SHE hands the book to RICK. HE starts browsing through it.)

JANET. Rick?

RICK. Yep?

JANET. Are you married?

RICK. Four years now.

JANET. What do you think?

RICK. About what?

JANET. Marriage.

RICK. Hm. Never thought about it.

JANET. Did it change your whole entire life?

RICK. No.

JANET. What's it like? Marriage?

RICK. *(Looking up from the book.)* Well, it can be the scariest
thing ever . . . but so can some of the lunch specials my cousin
serves in her dinette.

(JEFFREY enters. HE leaves the door open and leans back.

JANET crosses to close the door.)

JANET. Honey?

JEFFREY. *(Taking off his coat and scarf, shoes, loosening his tie, fixing a drink, etc.)* Rick, help yourself to the bar, the VCR, and my collection of "Greatest Hits" records. Take off your jacket. Stay awhile. *(HE collapses onto the couch.)*

JANET. *(To Jeffrey.)* Couldn't find your wallet, dear?

JEFFREY. Oh yes. Right there. On the dashboard. I knew it would be there, because I remember taking it out so I could tip the valet at the restaurant.

JANET. Yes?

JEFFREY. I also remember giving the man my last ten dollars. All I've got left is . . .

RITA. *(Entering.)* Can we please pass the pie?

JEFFREY. . . . my keycard to the fitness room. Hey, Rita. What kind of cash do you have?

RITA. Oh, great. I have to pay?!! I did not come here to be abused.

JEFFREY. Don't get all bent up. I'm broke—from dinner, the valet, *(To Janet.)* I think I bought you a couple of roses beforehand, didn't I?

JANET. You're so sweet.

RITA. *(Crying.)* Nobody's bought me roses since Howard Schupler. And I made him do it, too. But everyone else's dates got them flowers. I picked out two dead roses, a tub of chocolate ice cream and went through express. I'm sure if there was a parking space, the stupid duck would've bought buds. But he didn't.

(Silence. EVERYONE sits down. Even RICK. After a beat.)

RICK. *(To Jeffrey.)* You paid some guy ten bucks to park your car?

JEFFREY. He just went and got it for me. Some other guy actually parked it.

RICK. You tip *him*, too?

(JEFFREY nods.)

    RICK. I gotta get another job.
    JANET. What do you *want* to be doing?
    JEFFREY. Janet, what are you? His career counselor?!!
    RITA. But he's got the pizza.
    JANET. —and so much potential.
    JEFFREY. Agh!!!
    JANET. *(Pulling out her wallet.)* Take my card, Jeffrey. Go to the money machine.
    JEFFREY. Your machine's way out in Glendale.
    RICK. Hey, the store's in Freemont. Bring the money by. Give you a chance to meet Rick. See about a job.
    JANET. Jeffrey.
    JEFFREY. O.K. Fine. I'll do whatever you want. I'll go to Alaska to get money if that's what you want. I just want to be alone with you.

(JANET helps him with his coat and scarf, and gives him a kiss on the cheek.)

    RICK. Bye, Jeff.

(JEFFREY looks at Rick and exits.)

    RITA. Now I'm really depressed. (*SHE tries to get the pizza once again.*)
    RICK. Lady, I told you.

(RITA starts to exit.)

    JANET. Rita, where are you—
    RITA. To the all-night Mongolian take-out place and then home.
    RICK. Excuse me, but it's not like I'm tired of holding the pizzas or anything but all this talk about *not* eating is making me

really hungry.

RITA. Have a piece, Rick. You delivered it.

RICK. No. Eating your own delivery. That's bogus.

JANET. Oh. Wait. Rick, do you want some rice? There's rice on the stove.

RICK. Great. I was going to ask you if you had some rice, but I didn't think you had.

(RITA starts to exit. JANET stops her.)

JANET. *(To Rita.)* Don't go. I beg you. Jeffrey will be back soon. He'll pay Rick, and Rick will be gone. And you'll eat and then you'll be gone. And Jeffrey and I will be alone.

RITA. So?

JANET. I can't be alone with him.

RITA. Do you love him?

JANET. I do. I do. God, I do.

RITA. Then say "yes."

JANET. I can't.

RITA. Then say "no."

JANET. I can't.

RICK. That's it. There's nothing else.

RITA. Well, she could say "What, are you kidding?"

RICK. Hey, that's great. That doesn't say either. I mean, you can't tell *what* she means.

RITA. Leave him guessing for the next twenty years.

JANET. I want to get married. But not yet.

RITA. Then say that. "Not yet."

JANET. But then what?

RITA. What do you mean?

JANET. What's he going to do what when I tell him "not yet"? What's he going to do? Is that going to be O.K.? Is he going to be alright about that?

RICK. Who knows?

RITA. *(To Rick.)* Gimme a slice. Please?

(RICK shakes his head no.)

RITA. Pretty please?

(RICK shakes his head "no" again.)

RITA. I gotta have some!
RICK. No!

(RITA lunges at the pizza boxes. A struggle ensues. JANET pulls RITA off.)

RITA. I'm sorry. It's been a rough night. A miserable night.
JANET. What happened? I thought you went to a single's lecture.
RITA. I did.
JANET. How was it?
RITA. I met a guy over baklava.
RICK. You met someone. That's nice.
JANET. Are you going to see him again?
RITA. We gave each other our numbers. He mentioned to me there'd be a lecture next week. He's planning to go.
JANET. Sounds like he wants to see you again.
RITA. Right. And tell me more about his passing kidney stone.
RICK. My wife makes up songs with her teeth.
JANET. She what?
RICK. Popular tunes, too. *(HE clicks his teeth together.)* That's "You're a Grand Old Flag." *(RICK clicks his teeth together once again.)* "Amazing Grace." She does that one much better. *(HE goes back to his play.)*
RITA. How weird.
RICK. *(Reading.)* "Oh! if I wake, shall I not be distraught. Environed with all these hideous fears, and madly play with my forefathers' joints . . ." Fooling around with another person's elbow . . . now *that's* weird.
JANET. It's all so scary, you know?
RICK. Ruletta Bongo. She played Juliet. She got so scared when Romeo drank the poison. She liked him—like for real. But it

was only colored water. I know. I set it up. No way is he gonna die from it . . . No way!

JANET. Rick, I'll get you some rice. (*JANET exits.*)

RITA. I'm sorry I attacked you. I was hungry. I was depressed. Are you sure you don't want to sit down?

RICK. I can't. Rule.

RITA. What about music?

RICK. What about it?

RITA. Any rule against music?

RICK. Well, Jeffrey did tell me I could help myself to his collection of "Greatest Hits" records.

RITA. Well, hey. Let's go!

(*RITA puts on a classic rock n' roll tune from the "Greatest Hits" collection of a popular rock n' roll singer. SHE starts dancing. RICK really gets into it. HE finally lets go of the pizzas; RITA takes them from him, puts them down on the coffee table, and finally helps herself to a slice. HE takes off his jacket, and throws it across the room à la Chippendale. JANET enters with a bowl of rice. SHE is shocked, but smiles. RITA encourages her and so does RICK. ALL THREE are dancing around the living room. RITA passes out the pizza. THEY are spinning, twisting, and twirling all over the living room until finally RITA spins RICK too hard and too uncontrollably. HE lands right on top of the pizza. HE sits face front, feeling his backside bathed in tomato sauce. JANET goes to turn off the MUSIC.*)

RICK. The boss is gonna wonder.

RITA. I push guys too far.

RICK. I still had fun.

RITA. Better get out of those jeans.

JANET. Go into Jeff's room. Help yourself. Pants, bathrobe, whatever you need.

RICK. God, everyone around here is so nice. (*HE exits into the bedroom.*)

RITA. What are you going to do?

JANET. I need some air. I'm going for a walk.

RITA. It's late and this neighborhood . . .
JANET. I'll stick to the hallway.

(JANET crosses to the door, opens it. A POLICE OFFICER is standing at the door, holding JEFFREY who's wearing a jacket and cap from "Rick's Pizza." The OFFICER is snacking on licorice.)

OFFICER. Found him around the side trying to break in.
JEFFREY. I knocked but no one answered. What the hell were you playing, anyway?

(RICK enters wearing Jeffrey's bathrobe.)

RICK. *(To Jeffrey.)* Hey, Jeffrey, you look great.
JEFFREY. Your god-damn boss tried to sell me a Rick's key ring, a Rick's pen and pencil set, and a god-damn Rick's lunchbox. I was lucky to get out of there alive.
RICK. So? Did you pay for the pizza?
JEFFREY. Rick, I—why are you wearing my robe?
RICK. *(To Officer.)* What's the problem, sir?
OFFICER. Attempted burglary. Possible suicide. *(To everyone.)* Licorice, anyone?

(RITA goes for some. HE then pulls out a bag of M&M's.)

RICK. *(To Officer.)* Suicide? When'd that happen?
OFFICER. Oh. Well . . . I didn't hurry. I mean, the dispatcher . . . she was . . . she was . . . laughing. Laughing all the way through the call. I didn't feel . . . well . . . like I should've been in a real hurry or anything. *(To Rita.)* M & M?

(RITA helps herself to M & M's.)

RICK. Hey, that's serious. Someone about to do suicide. It deserves your immediate attention.
OFFICER. *(Licking his fingers.)* Yes, sir.

RITA. Wow! I'm impressed. All of a sudden . . . you're like
a . . . different delivery.

RICK. It's the robe, man. It's Jeff's robe. Thanks, big guy.

*(JEFFREY breaks free of the police officer, throws off his jacket
and cap, and is about to go for Rick as JANET breaks in.)*

JANET. Let's have some pizza, everyone!

RITA. *(Moving towards the Officer.)* Yeah. Come on.

RICK. There's Coke, too.

JANET. I'll get glasses.

RITA. We need more napkins.

OFFICER. Looks great.

RICK. Music. What kind of music do officers of the law . . . get
into?

JEFFREY. HOLD IT! EVERYBODY FREEZE! *(Quietly and
calmly.)* I have a request. If it's not too much trouble. Could all of
you please . . . GET THE HELL OUT OF HERE SO I CAN
FUCKING PROPOSE TO THIS WOMAN THAT I LOVE!!!

JANET. *(Pause.)* Jeffrey. All these people. Couldn't you have
waited until we were alone?

JEFFREY. Forget it. Just forget it.

JANET. Jeffrey?

JEFFREY. *(Eating a piece of pizza.)* I wanted too much. I
expected too much. *(To everybody.)* I wanted this to be the most
beautiful, romantic night in Janet's life. Why? I don't know. Yes, I
do. Because—except for tonight—she's made me the happiest guy
in the world. I mean—I love her. And—except for tonight—she's
turned my head about marriage. And—except for tonight—I've
been thinking lately about how I want to be with her for the rest of
my life. *(Down on one knee.)* C'mon, Janet. Marry me.

(ALL look on.)

JANET. But I don't know what to do. I don't know.

JEFFREY. *(Picks up the pizza jacket HE threw down before
and puts it on.)* Where's that stupid hat?

(JANET picks up the hat.)

JEFFREY. Give it to me, Janet.

JANET. Don't leave.

JEFFREY. But you said "no."

JANET. No.

JEFFREY. Then you'll marry me?

JANET. No.

JEFFREY. Give me the hat.

JANET. Don't you see?

JEFFREY. What? That you won't marry me? What's to see? "No" is "no."

JANET. No. "No" isn't "yes."

JEFFREY. Yes, I know.

JANET. But it's not "no."

JEFFREY. It's not?

JANET. No.

JEFFREY. Then what is it?

JANET. I don't know.

JEFFREY. What do you want?

JANET. It's not that.

JEFFREY. Then what?

JANET. It's what I *don't* want?

JEFFREY. Then what? What is it? What? What is it you *don't* want?

JANET. I don't want to lose you. I don't want you to leave.

JEFFREY. Why would I leave? I live here. And I love you.

JANET. But I'm not ready yet.

RICK and RITA. So?

JANET. Don't I have to be ready?

RICK and RITA. No.

JANET. Don't I have to know?

RICK and RITA. No.

JEFFREY. All you have to do is tell me what you want. Tell me what you need.

(JANET looks at Rita.)

RITA. Don't look at me.

(JANET looks at Rick.)

RICK. It's the robe, man.
JANET. *(Pause.)* Jeffrey. I want you to wait for me. The truth is . . . I don't feel ready yet.
JEFFREY. But I do.
JANET. Do you love me?

(HE nods.)

JANET. Then wait.
JEFFREY. But lights, music, ring. Those are the directions.
JANET. Honey, I'm not a bottle of mouthwash and you're not a tube of toothpaste.
OFFICER. *(Looking up from his notepad.)* How's that?
JANET. We'll get married, Jeffrey.
JEFFREY. When?
JANET. When I'm ready. When I am good and ready. I'll let you know.
JEFFREY. *(Sarcastic.)* How romantic.

(JEFFREY sulks. JANET puts the "Rick's Pizza" hat on Jeffrey's head.)

JANET. How sexy.

(THEY kiss. EVERYBODY looks away. EVERYBODY looks up. JANET and JEFFREY are still kissing. RICK goes into the bedroom. RITA takes another piece of pizza. The OFFICER does so, as well. RICK comes out of the bedroom, carrying his jacket and pants, wearing the robe, and his sneakers.)

RICK. *(To Rita, referring to his robe.)* Think they'd mind?

RITA. Do you need it?

(RICK takes off the robe. HE is in his underwear. HE puts on his "Rick's Pizza" jacket. HE carefully lays the robe on the back of the sofa.)

RITA. Those pants. Get to them right away. You don't want that stuff to settle. It'll never come out if you wait too long . . .

(RICK and RITA exit.)

OFFICER. Excuse me. Sir? Miss?

(JEFFREY and JANET are still kissing.)

OFFICER. Just wondering . . . Can I have another slice?

(THEY do not notice him as HE helps himself.)

OFFICER. It's excellent pizza. I mean—usually I get pepperoni but extra cheese is good too, unless of course you're watching your cholesterol which I happen to be . . . *(LIGHTS start to fade)* . . . do you have any Parmesan? I know. That's just more cheese but, hey, you only live once . . .

BLACKOUT

THE END

COSTUMES

JEFFREY: sports coat, slacks, overcoat, scarf, "Rick's Pizza" jacket, "Rick's Pizza" cap

JANET: semi-formal evening clothes, coat, purse

RICK: jacket with "Rick's Pizza" on the back and on cap, bathrobe

RITA: sweater, slacks

OFFICER: uniform

PROPS

telephone
ring
ring box
magazines
pens
pencils
clips
crumpled pieces of paper
socks
underwear
spoons
paperback books
coupons
tape player, tapes
2 wallets
1 money card
1 bag of chips
1 bag of licorice
1 bag of M&M's
1 copy of Shakespeare's *Romeo & Juliet*
2 pizzas
2 pizza boxes
1 insulated pizza jacket
pizza bill

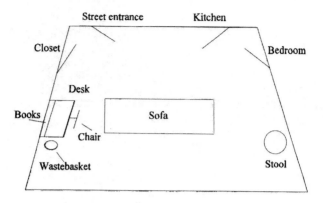

Note that door flats can be eliminated with the use of two upstage corner flats which suggest corridors leading right and left for the four exits, but that there is a great deal to be gained in the sense of farce if we can see the actual entrances and exits as they happen.

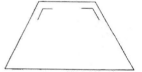

JULIANNE BERNSTEIN's plays have been produced in Philadelphia, Milwaukee, Washington, D.C. and at Actors Theatre of Louisville. In New York, her plays have appeared in the Five and Dime Festival, Women's Workshop, and every year since 1991 in the Annual Off-Off Broadway Short Play Festival. She is the winner of the 1984 Avery Hopwood Award, the Dogwood National One-Act, the Association of Theater and Higher Education, the Society of Arts and Letters' National Teleplay Competitions, and was a finalist in the 1993 George R. Kernodle Competition and Chesterfield/Film Writers Project. Ms. Bernstein's *Autumn Leaves* appears in *Off-Off Broadway Festival Plays: 16th Series* and additional plays appear in *More One-Act Plays for Acting Students*. Ms. Bernstein was commissioned by Theater Ariel in Philadelphia where her play, *Single Jewish Female* was produced at the Walnut Street Studio Theater. She has been a playwright-in-residence at the Mount Sequoyah New Play Retreat and a director/dramaturg at the Shenandoah New Play Retreat. Ms. Bernstein serves as Playwright-in-Residence for the Outreach Programs at McCarter Theater, and the Philadelphia Young Playwrights Festival, and has taught for George Street Playhouse and the New York Shakespeare Festival's Playwrights-in-the-Schools Program in residence at the Public Theater. She holds her M.F.A. in Playwriting from Rutgers University.